D1012158

FROM THE
NANCY DREW FILES

THE CASE: Nancy investigates the five-year-old death of a screen star on the romantic isle of Tahiti.

CONTACT: Bree Gordon, daughter of the dead star Lucinda Prado, calls Nancy for help after receiving three strange letters.

SUSPECTS: Kristin Stromm—*the glamorous and ambitious actress is engaged to Bree's famous father— but she has a secret.*

Brian Gordon—*the hot-tempered director had a fight with his wife the night she died.*

Rupert Holmberg—*the powerful film producer made three million dollars from Lucinda's death.*

COMPLICATIONS: Nancy's key evidence comes from a dead man!

Books in THE NANCY DREW FILES® Series

Available from ARCHWAY paperbacks

THE NANCY DREW FILES™ CASE · 31

TROUBLE IN TAHITI

Carolyn Keene

AN ARCHWAY PAPERBACK
Published by POCKET BOOKS
New York   London   Toronto   Sydney   Tokyo

This book is a work of fiction. Names, characters, places and incidents are either the product of the author's imagination or are used fictitiously. Any resemblance to actual events or locales or persons, living or dead, is entirely coincidental.

AN ARCHWAY PAPERBACK *Original*

An Archway Paperback published by
POCKET BOOKS, a division of Simon & Schuster Inc.
1230 Avenue of the Americas, New York, NY 10020

ISBN: 0-671-64698-2

First Archway Paperback printing January 1989

10 9 8 7 6 5 4 3 2 1

NANCY DREW, AN ARCHWAY PAPERBACK and colophon
are registered trademarks of Simon & Schuster Inc.

THE NANCY DREW FILES is a trademark
of Simon & Schuster Inc.

Printed in the U.S.A.

IL 7+

TROUBLE
IN TAHITI

Chapter

One

NANCY DREW PEERED into the tennis court through the chain-link fence, feeling the warmth of Tahiti's tropical sun on her face. Even though this was strictly a working vacation, she couldn't help but look forward to returning to wintry River Heights with a golden tan.

On the court two women volleyed back and forth. One, a pretty girl of nineteen with long, raven black hair, walloped the ball over the net with a sharp backhand.

Her opponent, a stunningly beautiful blond woman, rushed forward but was a split second too late. The ball bounced twice on the clay.

The black-haired girl grinned. "That's the game, Krissy."

Pouting, the blonde shouldered her racket. "Just wait till tomorrow, Bree Gordon."

Nancy intercepted the black-haired girl at the gate. "Bree? I'm Nancy Drew."

"Hi!" Bree shook Nancy's hand. "You made it. Did you have a nice flight to Papeete?"

Nancy noticed how easily the difficult Tahitian word rolled off the girl's lips: *Pah-pee-ay-tee.*

"A nice long flight." Nancy shook her head ruefully. "Eight hours from L.A.!"

Bree nodded knowingly, then gestured at her companion. "Let me introduce you. This is my father's fiancée, Kristin Stromm. Krissy, this is Nancy Drew."

As Nancy shook the blond woman's hand, she thought with an inward smile how jealous her star-struck friend Bess Marvin would be. Kristin Stromm was one of the most popular actresses in Hollywood.

"Pleased to meet you." Kristin's speech betrayed the soft tones of her native Sweden. "Bree darling, I have to run. The masseur's expecting me in ten minutes."

Bree arched her brows. "Okay. If I see Dad, I'll tell him you're in the body shop."

Nancy noticed the mask of annoyance that suddenly descended upon the older woman's face.

Kristin frowned. "Must you always have the last word?"

"Hey, lighten up, Krissy. It was only a joke."

"I don't think it was very amusing." Kristin

2

pushed open the chain-link gate. "Perhaps I ought to have a word with your father."

"Be my guest." Bree flashed a sassy smile. *"Haere maru."*

After the older woman strode away, Nancy said politely, "Uh, perhaps I came at an awkward time."

Bree's expression was apologetic. "Sorry. I didn't mean to drag you into anything. It's just that sometimes things get a little tense between me and my future stepmother." She frowned, watching Kristin enter the lobby of the luxurious Hotel Taravao. "I wish I knew what Dad sees in her."

Nancy tactfully tried to change the subject. "Bree, what was that you said a moment ago?"

"Haere maru. It's Tahitian for 'take it easy.'" Bree led Nancy through the hotel's garden, alive with exotic flowers in bright colors. "The language is practically second nature to me. I used to live here every summer when I was younger. And, of course, Tayo taught me a lot."

"Who's Tayo?" Nancy inquired.

"Tayo Kapali." Bree's face clouded. "He's the reason I asked you to come."

"What *exactly* is the problem? Let's go over it once. Okay?"

Bree nodded. "At first I thought it was a joke. But when it happened three times . . ." After taking a deep breath, Bree went on. "Somebody keeps sending weird letters to my dorm."

3

"Could you describe the letters?" Nancy asked, prompting her.

"They're crazy!" Bree's pretty face tightened angrily. "Always the same little remark. 'You'd be surprised if you knew what I know about your mother's death.'"

Nancy experienced a shiver of disgust. What a cruel thing to write. No wonder Bree was so upset.

"Anyway, the person's dead wrong," Bree added. "There was nothing suspicious about my mother's death. If anything, it was the most publicized boating accident in the history of the Pacific."

Nancy's mind drifted back twenty-four hours to the time of the two phone calls she had received—one from an old client, Alice Faulkner, who was Bree's godmother, the other from Bree herself. Mrs. Faulkner had given her a few of the details, but Nancy hadn't needed much prompting to recall the accident that had claimed one of Hollywood's biggest stars. "Was that five years ago?"

"Yeah." Bree pushed open the hotel's glass doors. "My parents owned a boat back then. The *Southwind,* a custom-built motor sailer. She went down in a tropical storm with my mother aboard. There was a crewman aboard, too, a guy named Pierre Panchaud." Bree swallowed hard. Unhappy memories brought tears to her brown eyes.

"How did it happen?" Nancy asked softly.

"The *Southwind* lost her anchor during the storm and drifted into the main shipping channel. A tramp freighter rammed her. M-Mother died in the wreck." Bree hastily wiped at her eye. "The local maritime board investigation declared it a simple, unavoidable accident." She took a deep breath. "Gosh, look at me. You'd think I'd be over it by now."

"You never really get over a tragedy like that, Bree." Nancy touched the girl's shoulder sympathetically. "I know. I lost my mother when I was three."

"I'm sorry," Bree murmured.

Nancy changed the subject as Bree led her past a bank of public elevators to a smaller one marked Private. "Let's concentrate on this letter writer. Tell me, where were the anonymous letters mailed from?"

"That's what's *really* strange. They all came from Tahiti." Bree halted at the door to the elevator and slipped a key out of her pocket. After unlocking the door, she continued. "I haven't been here in four years. All my old friends are grown up and gone. Nobody even knew I was going to UCLA."

"Where does Tayo come into it?" Nancy asked, searching for any connection.

"Tayo used to be the *Southwind*'s chief mate. He taught me to scuba dive." The girls stepped inside, and Bree pushed the only button. "Tayo knows practically everybody on the island. I

figured he could help me track down the weirdo."
A worried look crossed her face. "But I can't find
Tayo *anywhere*. He didn't return my calls, and no
one I asked had seen him. When I went to his
house, it was all boarded up, as if he'd left a long
time ago. I started to investigate myself, but I got
a creepy feeling, as if somebody was watching
me. I got scared."

The elevator doors opened suddenly, exposing
a plush penthouse suite. Tropical plants hung
from metal flowerpots. Stylish teak furniture
filled the room. Huge windows offered panoram-
ic views of Papeete's sky-blue harbor and the
jungly neighboring island of Moorea.

"Bree, could I have a look at one of those
letters?" Nancy asked.

"Sure. This way." Bree beckoned with her
hand.

Nancy followed her into a spacious bedroom.
A four-poster bed, covered with a lightweight
quilt, dominated the peach-colored room. An
empty plastic shoe tree stood beside the highly
polished dresser.

Bree opened the dresser's top drawer and
pulled out three air mail envelopes.

"Here. Except for Auntie Alice, I haven't told
anyone about them." Bree handed them to Nancy, then seated herself on the bed. "I didn't want
to upset Dad and Krissy, especially with their
wedding coming up."

Nancy flipped through them, noting the Tahiti

postmarks and French stamps. Then she withdrew one of the letters and unfolded it.

The paper was lined notebook stuff, available in any stationery store. It was the rigid lettering that perked Nancy's interest. She frowned thoughtfully.

"What is it?" asked Bree.

"Whoever wrote these took the trouble to disguise their handwriting. The letters are formed with a pen and ruler. There's no way a handwriting expert could even tell who wrote them," Nancy said, her mind racing.

Bree's face fell. "Then they're no help."

"Actually, they're a big help." Nancy's dimpled smile came quick to reassure Bree. "They tell me that the writer is someone you know. He or she was afraid you'd recognize the handwriting. That explains the ruler."

Turning to return the letters to Bree, Nancy spied a sudden movement underneath the bedspread. She froze. Something narrow was gliding along, moving steadily toward Bree.

Nancy thrust out her hand. "Don't move!"

The girl blinked. "What?"

"Keep still," Nancy whispered, rounding the edge of the bed. Her hand gripped the coverlet. "When I throw this back, hop off the bed—fast!"

Puzzled, Bree nodded.

Nancy whispered, "One—two—"

"Three!" Heart thumping, Nancy ripped the coverlet away. A hiss filled the air.

7

A gleaming black snake lay on the mattress. Bree gasped and leaped off the bed.

Baring its fangs, the snake rose on its coils, ready to strike.

And Nancy was standing right in front of it!

Chapter
Two

H*ISSSSS!* FANGS DRIPPING VENOM, the snake weaved from side to side.

Nancy swallowed hard. Slowly she moved her head to the left. The snake's wedge-shaped head darted in that direction. Seeing her chance, Nancy lashed out with her other hand and seized the deadly serpent right behind its head.

A deft flick of her wrist sent it hurtling into the corner. The snake rolled on the rug, stunned. Nancy grabbed the shoe tree and used the prongs to pin the snake to the carpet.

"Call hotel security, Bree."

Thick plastic hooks kept the snake trapped as it wriggled helplessly, wrapping itself into a coil.

Nancy knew she was safe, but she'd be more pleased to be on the safe side of glass observing the slippery reptile in a zoo.

Bree rushed to the telephone, grabbed the receiver, and tapped the *O* button. "This is Bree Gordon in the penthouse. There's a snake loose up here! Help us!"

Nancy kept up the pressure on the shoe tree. The snake's beady eyes gleamed; its flailing tail just missed her arm.

Suddenly Nancy heard a woman's voice behind her.

"Bree?"

Turning her head, Nancy saw an attractive chestnut-haired woman in a crisp lilac linen suit standing in the doorway. "What's going on here?"

The newcomer's gaze traveled from Bree to Nancy to the snake. Then her face went white, her eyes rolled upward, and she slid to the carpet like a dress off a hanger.

Bree hung up the phone. "Oh, Manda!"

"I hope you can take care of her." Nancy glanced at the writhing snake. "I'm a little occupied at the moment."

Bree knelt beside the unconscious woman. Two minutes later the hotel manager and two khaki-clad security guards bustled into the suite. Nancy was grateful when one of them took over the snake-guarding duty from her. The other slipped a snare's noose around the snake's neck and toted it away.

Nancy helped Bree and the manager move Manda onto the bed. The manager patted her wrist repeatedly, uttering apologies in high-speed French.

Nancy soaked a facecloth in the bathroom. "Is she a friend of yours, Bree?"

"Not quite. Manda's practically family."

Bree explained that Amanda Withers was her father's executive secretary. She had worked for film director Brian Gordon since Bree was in junior high school.

Returning to the bedroom, Nancy delicately placed the facecloth on Manda's brow. The woman moaned softly. Her eyes fluttered open.

"Bree?" Her face fearful, Manda sat up and embraced the girl. "Bree, are you all right? That snake—"

"I'm fine, Manda." Bree tried to disengage herself from Manda's frantic hug.

"Are you certain?" Seated on the edge of the bed, Manda squeezed Bree's arms and shoulders as an anxious mother would examine a bruised child.

Nancy thought Bree looked terribly embarrassed by Manda's performance.

"Look, I'm *fine,*" Bree said, standing abruptly. "Why don't you go with the manager? The house doctor can have a look at you."

"Please, madame, this way." The manager put out his arm to guide Manda to the elevator.

After their departure Bree shook her head wryly. "Manda Mother Hen." A crooked smile

11

wrinkled her mouth. "Honestly, that woman thinks I'm still eleven years old."

Nancy said nothing, but she had already arrived at the same obvious conclusion. Manda was trying very hard to be Bree's substitute mother—perhaps a bit too hard.

Bree rubbed her arms briskly. "Ugh! When I think about that snake! . . ."

"Bree, I think somebody just tried to kill you," Nancy said, keeping her voice low. "Snakes don't ride elevators and hide under bedspreads. Somebody must have put it there!"

"But *why?*"

"It's possible that the letter writer knows you're after him," Nancy added.

"How can that be? I didn't come up with a single clue. I couldn't even find Tayo."

"Maybe your search made him nervous," Nancy said thoughtfully. "Tell me what you've done so far."

"Well . . ." Bree chewed her thumbnail. "I came across something while I was trying to find Tayo. A friend of mine saw Tayo's boat two years ago. Only it didn't belong to Tayo anymore. I was planning to check the records to see who owns it."

"If you don't mind, I'd like to pursue that line of inquiry myself." Inspiration made Nancy's eyes glimmer. "What was the name of Tayo's boat?"

"The *Rapanui.*" She watched Nancy head for the elevator. "Where are you going?"

Pressing the button, Nancy said, "Bree, I need you to talk to the concierge to see if you can casually find out who came up to the suite today. All right?"

Bree nodded. "No problem," she said.

"Good. Now, can you tell me where they keep the town's official records?"

"Government center, I guess. The gendarmerie is right downtown, just off the Boulevard Pomare."

"Thanks! I'll be back."

After picking up her rental-car keys at the front desk, Nancy went to her own suite and changed her travel clothes for a white tank top and a pair of mint green shorts. Boat clothes, she decided, would keep her cool and comfortable in Tahiti's sweltering climate.

Nancy made certain that her maroon Renault had a road map and a first-aid kit in the glove compartment. Then, after a hasty survey of the map, she drove downtown.

The government center was right on Papeete's sparkling waterfront. Sea birds shrieked at passing yachts. Gentle waves rolled ashore on a beach of black volcanic sand. Nancy was grateful for the refreshing offshore breeze.

The French tricolor rippled from the flagpole. Nancy remembered that Tahiti and her neighboring islands were part of French Polynesia, a self-governing island territory of France.

A wizened old man with a gap-toothed grin

directed Nancy to the maritime office. She hoped her years of French at River Heights High would be enough to make herself understood.

Fortunately, the clerk had no trouble understanding Nancy.

"I'm afraid there is no longer an active safety permit for the *Rapanui*," he said, showing Nancy an official document. "The boat was sold for scrap two years ago."

"Was it sold by Tayo Kapali?" she asked.

"No, mademoiselle, that is not the name on the bill of sale."

That's odd, Nancy mused. Why hadn't Tayo sold the boat?

"Could you tell me who bought the boat, monsieur?"

"It was purchased by Ruau's scrap yard. Just down the beach."

"Thank you." Flashing him a grateful smile, Nancy picked up her shoulder bag and strode away, eager to pursue her first lead.

Leaving her Renault in the parking lot, Nancy joined the flow of pedestrians heading for the beach. Her gaze encompassed all the strikingly different people walking the sands: tourists in sunglasses and straw hats, Frenchmen in knit shirts and faded jeans, breathtakingly lovely Tahitian girls in cool-looking sundresses.

Ruau's scrap yard was just beyond the main boat basin, a field of wooden hulls upended on top of trestles. An old-fashioned steam crane crouched beside the wharves, a plume of smoke drifting from its stack, its engine grumbling ceaselessly.

A workman pointed out the owner, Arii Ruau. Nancy saw a rawboned Tahitian in his early forties, with a tough, shrewd expression.

"Monsieur Ruau, do you remember a boat named the *Rapanui?*" Nancy inquired after she had introduced herself.

"Why, yes, I bought it two years ago." Ruau made an impatient motion with his right hand. "I wanted to refit it, but the bottom was too far gone. So I scrapped the *Rapanui.* A pity, eh?"

"Do you know a man named Tayo Kapali?"

Ruau frowned, then shook his head. "No, the name is not familiar."

"Tayo used to own the *Rapanui* four years ago," Nancy added.

"That's possible." Ruau shrugged. "Boats change hands quite often here in Tahiti. I bought it from Temeharo."

"Who's he?" she asked, trying not to sound too curious.

"A fisherman. He lives on the south side of the island. I can tell you where to find him."

"I'd appreciate that."

Nancy listened attentively as the owner gave her directions to Temeharo's village. As he was talking, she heard the crane's engine suddenly pick up speed.

Nancy was about to ask him to raise his voice

when something caught her eye. She spied a long, thin shadow moving ominously toward them over the sand.

In a flash she realized what it was—the crane's upright boom.

Nancy's gaze lifted, and her suspicion was confirmed. The long steel-girdered boom had drifted into position above their heads. With a metallic creak, it came to a halt.

The rust-dappled scoop, brimming with scrap, swung lazily back and forth.

The scoop's steel hinges groaned suddenly. The noise prickled the hairs on the back of Nancy's neck.

The scoop's jaws were opening!

Nancy's eyes blinked wide.

Its hinges screaming, the scoop opened and let loose its load of jagged steel scrap.

Chapter

Three

Look out!" Nancy screamed.

Grabbing Ruau's shoulders, she shoved him backward. They hit the sand together. Still holding on, Nancy rolled with him beneath an overturned whaleboat.

Steel fragments bombarded the sand. A handful of shrapnel hammered the boat above their heads. When the noise had stopped, Nancy lay still for a moment, shaken by the close call. If it hadn't been for the whaleboat's hull . . . Nancy shook her head slowly. After a minute she peeked out. The empty scoop spun at the end of its cable. Steel scrap littered the sand.

The workers came running. One helped Nancy to her feet.

Ashen faced, Ruau tottered upright. Brushing off the sand, he yelled, "Imbeciles! You almost killed me! Who was running that crane?"

A confused babble of voices broke out as the workers pointed accusatory fingers at one another. Ruau waded into the crowd and began berating them all. Nancy glanced quickly at the crane itself. The cab was empty. Farther down the beach, a cabin cruiser lolled in its berth.

Nancy cautiously climbed the crane's caterpillar treads. A quick check of the cab confirmed her hunch. The scoop hadn't been opened accidentally. Its jaws were locked with a hydraulic valve that had to be turned by hand.

After jumping down from the cab, Nancy carefully checked the ground on the opposite side. Two deep footprints marked the turf. Kneeling, she examined the treads' pattern more closely.

Diamond-shaped indentations filled each print. Nancy frowned in recognition. Boat shoes! That tread gave sailors better traction on a wet deck.

Hmmm, she thought. Someone climbed into that cab, swung the boom toward us, and opened the scoop. Then he jumped to the ground, leaving those two deep prints, and hightailed it out of here.

"Mademoiselle, what are you doing?" Ruau appeared at the crane, flanked by excited workmen.

Nancy's eyes quickly scanned everyone's feet.

No boat shoes. They were all wearing construction boots.

"You saved my life." Ruau squeezed Nancy's hand thankfully. "If not for you, these idiots—"

"Don't blame your men. They're not responsible," Nancy interrupted. She hurriedly explained her deduction.

Concern tightened Ruau's features. "Maybe we'd better call the police."

"First let's check out that boat," Nancy suggested, pointing at the nearby cabin cruiser. "Maybe someone on it saw something."

As they strode toward the dock, the boat's engines roared to life. White water burbled around the stern. The cruiser pulled away casually, heading for the open sea. Shading her eyes against the sun's glare, Nancy caught a glimpse of its gilt-edged name: *Sous le Vent.*

Nancy smiled ruefully. "So much for that idea."

She watched the cruiser fade into the distance. Of course, it could merely be a coincidence that the boat's skipper had chosen that moment to depart. Her smile faded. Then again, whoever had tried to kill them could be on board, making an escape.

After saying goodbye to Ruau and his men, Nancy walked to the dockmaster's shed. The dockmaster was a sharp-nosed elderly Frenchman in a tattered tan beret and a flowered shirt. An unlit cigarette dangled from his lips.

Sudden inspiration caused Nancy to take a less

19

direct tack with the older man. She wondered if being too open in her quest for information could be dangerous.

"Excuse me," Nancy said, flashing her sweetest smile. "The boat that just pulled out of here—is it for sale?"

The dockmaster squinted out to sea. "Eh? The *Sous le Vent?* No, no, not for sale."

"Do you know who owns it?" asked Nancy. "Maybe I'll make him an offer, anyway."

"That's Chaumette's boat." Somehow he managed to talk around his cigarette. "Henri Chaumette."

Nancy thought. Chaumette. That name didn't ring any bells, but she filed it away for future reference.

After thanking the dockmaster, Nancy headed back to the gendarmerie. As she strolled along, she mulled over her first eventful day.

Were the two murder attempts connected? Whoever had planted that snake in Bree's bed could have seen Nancy with Bree. If that person had overheard their conversation about the anonymous letters, then he or she knew Nancy was a private investigator.

Suppose the would-be killer then followed Nancy to the gendarmerie and the scrap yard. Ruau's idling crane had offered the perfect opportunity to set up a phony accident.

Nancy's frown deepened as her thoughts returned to the *Sous le Vent.* Was it used to make an escape? Could Henri Chaumette be after her?

And, if so, what was his connection to Bree Gordon, or to Tayo Kapali?

Nancy began to wonder about the former chief mate. How did Tayo lose his boat two years ago? Most important, why had he dropped completely out of sight?

A cool sea breeze raised gooseflesh on Nancy's bare arms. The mystery, it seemed, went far deeper than a handful of hate-mail letters!

The next morning Nancy and Bree drove south to find the fisherman who'd sold Tayo's boat. Nancy steered the Renault down the Taapuna Highway, past the elegant mansions and lush ironwood groves of Tahiti's western shore. Beyond the sprawling estates the blue Pacific exploded into spray on the narrow rampart of a coral reef.

"What did you find out from the concierge yesterday?" Nancy asked her companion.

Bree frowned. "Nothing much. He said he didn't see anyone unusual go near our elevator yesterday. Just Dad, Krissy, and Manda—all family, more or less. But he wasn't watching the entire time. I got him to admit that he was back in his office, arguing with a crazy customer for about half an hour. So anyone could have gotten hold of a key and gone up during that time."

Right—or it could have been one of the "family," Nancy added mentally. But there was no point in voicing that possibility to Bree. It would only upset her.

"Did your friend Tayo ever mention an Henri Chaumette?" Nancy asked.

Shaking her head, Bree replied, "Not to me."

"What about your mother? Did she ever mention that name?"

"She might have. I honestly don't remember." Bree made a rueful face. "Mother knew just about everybody on the island. I think she wanted to be queen of Tahiti." She sighed nostalgically. "Mother was from Peru. She got her start in Rio, as a showgirl in one of the big nightclubs. By the time she was twenty-one, she was doing TV and movies. She hit it big in a low-budget comedy called *Coralita.* It established Mother as *the* biggest star in South America."

Nancy wasn't much of a Hollywood fan. But because Bess was, she did know a little about Lucinda Prado's career.

"Then she came to Hollywood and did *Shivaree* and *The Tall Timber,* right?" Nancy remarked.

"Yeah. Dad directed *Tall Timber.* That's how they met." Bree smiled impishly. "They got married the minute the film wrapped."

"How did you all wind up in Tahiti?"

"When I was a kid, Dad and Mother formed their own production company and did *Typhoon* down here," Bree explained. "That made tons of money, so they did a couple of sequels. Mother just fell in love with the island. Tahiti became our permanent vacation home."

Coconut palms flashed by on either side of the road. Nancy could understand just how Bree's mother felt. She glanced at her companion. "Sounds like an exciting life."

"Well—up to a point, yes." Bree turned serious. "Toward the end, though, Mother was fed up with the film industry. She was forty, and they were still casting her in Coralita parts. She wanted to prove that she was a serious actress. And I think maybe she was a little jealous of Dad's success."

Nancy caught an undertone of sadness in the girl's voice. "It got a little tense at home, huh?"

"A bit!" Bree said candidly. "When you've got two creative, opinionated people married to each other, you're bound to have friction. And Mother had a temper!" She exhaled deeply. "I got pretty good at disappearing at the first sign of tension."

Nancy thought it was time to change the subject. "We're heading inland again. How do we get back to the shore?"

"Oh!" Bree sat up attentively. "There's a dirt road just ahead. It goes right along the bay. The village is down there."

They found what they were looking for within five minutes. Temeharo's fish market was right on the beach, a long corrugated tin shed with a thatched roof. Fresh tuna and halibut rested on smoking blocks of dry ice.

Temeharo was a fiftyish man in a khaki shirt and oil-stained trousers. He flashed a gleaming

23

smile of welcome, and Nancy was instantly taken by his open, friendly manner. "Come in! How may I help you?"

"My name's Nancy Drew." Nancy shook hands with him. "And this is Bree Gordon. We're looking for a friend and thought you might be able to help. I understand you sold a boat two years ago—the *Rapanui.*"

"Yes, I sold her in Papeete."

"Did you buy it from Tayo Kapali?" asked Nancy.

His eyes gleamed in recognition. "No, not from Tayo himself."

"But you know of Tayo," Nancy added quickly.

The fisherman brightened. "Of course. He came from this village."

Mystified, Nancy asked, "Who did you buy the boat from?"

"The bank." Temeharo saw Nancy's confused look. "Tayo still owed money on her," the fisherman explained. "The bank foreclosed after his death."

Nancy blinked in amazement at this unexpected development.

"After his—"

"Yes, mademoiselle. Tayo is dead. He was killed four years ago."

Chapter

Four

No!" BREE CRIED, rushing forward. "That's not true. I talked to Tayo four years ago. He was alive."

Temeharo offered her a look of sympathy. "I'm sorry, but I saw his body with my own eyes. Tayo was killed in a shark attack." Nancy grimaced but pushed the gruesome thought from her mind.

"When did it happen?" she asked, placing a comforting arm around Bree's shoulder.

"October, I think," the fisherman replied.

Turning to Bree, Nancy added softly, "When did you last see Tayo?"

"A-August." Bree began to sob. "I—I had no idea . . . he . . . Tayo's *dead!*"

25

Nancy walked Bree back to the car. She opened a fresh package of tissues from the glove compartment and offered one to Bree. Temeharo came over to see if she was all right.

Nancy led him away from the car. Bree deserved a little privacy for her grief. And she still had a few questions for Temeharo.

"What's this about a shark attack?" Nancy asked.

Temeharo's smile was one of admiration. "Tayo was the best diver on the island. That was why everyone was so shocked when it happened to him." He glanced out to sea. "Tayo went diving off the *Rapanui* one afternoon. A few people claim they saw another boat out there too. Who knows? Suddenly, the people tell me, the water started to foam. Shark fins were everywhere. A couple of men in a canoe drove off the sharks with rifle fire. They brought Tayo in." He made a sudden sickish face. "Or rather what was left of him. Tayo must have cut himself on the coral down there. Sharks go crazy at the smell of blood, you know."

Nancy thought immediately of the two recent murder attempts. "Did the police consider foul play?"

Temeharo shook his head. "There was no way to tell. Those sharks didn't leave much for the coroner."

Nancy stared in dismay. The trail seemed to have come to an end. Without Tayo, unraveling the mystery of the anonymous letters would be much harder.

Nancy brightened a little at her next thought. *If I can't talk to Tayo, I'll talk to someone who knew Tayo very well.*

"Did Tayo have any relatives?" Nancy asked.

"Just one," Temeharo replied. "His sister, Opane. She lives up there on Orohena." The sweep of his hand took in most of a lofty mountain rising behind the village. "Just ask around. People will tell you how to find her."

"Thanks." Giving him a grateful smile, Nancy headed back to the car.

Bree's sobbing had subsided to sniffles. Dabbing at her eyes, she stared out the windshield as they drove back to Papeete.

Nancy tried to draw the girl out. She wanted to know more about Bree's friendship with Tayo. She was beginning to wonder if Tayo's death could be linked in any way to the recent close calls in the porthouse and at the scrap yard.

"What brought you back to Tahiti four years ago?" Nancy asked.

"Dad had a few legal matters to tie up." Bree crumpled the tissue in her fist. "I didn't really want to come—Mother's death was still fresh in my mind. I spent most of the time with Tayo. It was a rotten trip all around. Even Tayo seemed sort of—well, distant."

Nancy cast her a quick glance. "Distant? What do you mean?"

"Tayo had something on his mind," Bree recalled. "He didn't want to talk about it. He said he had to check something out first. He made me promise to look him up the next time I was in Tahiti."

"And then he died," Nancy concluded for her. "Bree, did Tayo ever mention his sister?"

Bree's brown eyes widened in surprise. "Tayo had a sister? I didn't know that."

"Mr. Temeharo says Tayo has a sister living up on Mount Orohena." Nancy steered the car around a long shoreside bend. "Shall we go tomorrow?"

"Sure!" Bree's smile reappeared.

Two hours later as the girls sauntered through the hotel lobby, the desk clerk lifted a white envelope and called out, "Message for you, Mademoiselle Gordon."

Bree ripped the envelope open and withdrew a folded note. She scanned it quickly, then smiled wryly.

"We're both invited to dinner at Krissy's place tonight. And we're not to come in jeans. What do you say, Nancy?"

Grinning, Nancy brushed her reddish blond hair back over her shoulder. Her blue eyes sparkled. "Sounds good to me. I've got an outfit for a special occasion."

Kristin's estate, Faretaha, dominated a small plateau overlooking the windswept sands of a private beach. The house was enormous, with the high windows and lacy woodwork of the French colonial period. Tall, graceful coconut palms shaded a tropical garden ablaze with white gardenias and orange hibiscus.

As Nancy paused before the door, turning to admire the purple streaks the sunset had painted in the sky, the romantic setting made her feel wistful for a moment. Into her mind flashed an image of Ned Nickerson, and she suddenly missed her boyfriend. If only he could have come with her!

Her reverie was short-lived however. Just then the door opened and a Tahitian servant conducted Nancy and Bree into the drawing room. Two men sat in comfortable wicker chairs. One was tall and tanned, his thinning brown hair flecked with gray. Horn-rimmed glasses and an aquiline nose gave him a professorial look. The other man was shorter, pasty faced, beady eyed, about fifty pounds heavier, and was wearing a wrinkled summerweight suit.

Bree hugged the man with the glasses. "Hi, Dad!"

"All through gallivanting, eh?" Brian Gordon stood up and took Nancy's hand. "You must be Ms. Drew."

"It's a pleasure, Mr. Gordon." Nancy was surprised to find his handshake frail and tentative. Although he put on an amiable front, Nancy sensed that he was intensely private, perhaps a

29

bit frightened of other people. "I saw *Canaveral* back home. I liked it very much," she offered.

The director looked pleased. "Thank you. Personally, I think it's my best."

The man in the wrinkled suit uttered a morose grunt. "It lost money."

Bree gestured toward him. "Nancy, this is Rupert Holmberg, a producer."

Standing, Rupert made a frame of his pudgy hands. "Bree, you're breaking my heart. Look at you. Lucinda all over again. Let me get you a film. Come and talk to me."

"Thanks, but no thanks, Rupert." Bree waved him aside, smiling indulgently. "I want to be a marine biologist, not an actress."

Brian flashed Nancy a look of paternal approval. "A girl with sense."

Then Nancy heard the tapping of high heels behind her. Turning, she saw Kristin Stromm glide through the doorway. The actress was wearing a shirred jade-colored cocktail dress—an original straight from Paris, Nancy guessed.

Smiling coldly at Bree, Kristin drawled, "I'm so glad you could come, dear. You and your friend—ah—"

"Nancy Drew," Bree added sweetly.

Nancy felt the air of tension between Bree and her future stepmother. She wondered why Kristin had bothered with such a petty routine. From the look in the actress's pale blue eyes, it was obvious that Kristin remembered Nancy's name. It was also clear that she wasn't exactly pleased with Nancy's appearance. A long-skirted, peach-colored evening dress highlighted Nancy's shining hair and hugged her trim figure.

A servant approached to announce dinner. Nancy enjoyed the French Polynesian delicacies— fresh fish marinated in coconut milk with smoked breadfruit and *fafa,* cooked Tahitian spinach, on the side.

While they ate, Nancy studied Bree's father. She had a few questions for the taciturn director. Nancy was determined to explore the connection between the letters Bree had received and what Tayo might have known about Lucinda's death.

She worked into it gradually, questioning Brian about his three *Typhoon* movies first. Then she mentioned the boat. "I guess you had the *Southwind* for quite a while, Mr. Gordon."

"Seven years." Brian sipped his coffee.

"Did you enjoy sailing?"

"Once in a while. Lucinda was crazy about it, though."

"I gather your wife was a very experienced sailor," Nancy commented.

"Oh, yes." Brian aimed a conspiratorial smile at his daughter. "Bree and I logged a lot of nautical miles under Captain Prado."

"It seems a bit strange—" Nancy began.

"What seems strange?" Brian adjusted his glasses.

"With your wife so experienced, I'm surprised

31

that freighter was able to run the *Southwind* down."

Brian's good mood vanished abruptly. Fixing Nancy with a frosty stare, he snapped, "I'd rather not talk about that, if you don't mind. My wife's death was a very great tragedy in my life. It's not something I discuss with strangers."

"I'm sorry," Nancy replied apologetically.

"No need to be sorry." Nancy noticed the sudden angry set of his lips. "Just drop it, okay?"

Taken aback by his snappish response, Nancy did not reply. But his overreaction intrigued her. Even if he was still sensitive about the mishap after five years, his reaction should have been sadness, not anger.

An awkward silence hung over the dinner table. Kristin smiled weakly, toying with an earring, and attempted to fill it.

"Darling," she said pleasantly, "I'm wondering if you've gotten those script rewrites yet for our new film."

Plucking an olive off the tray, Rupert popped it in his mouth. "Hey! Now we're talking. *South of the Equator*'s a potential gold mine. Brian, let me line up a few banks and a big-name cast."

Brian looked weary. "Rupert, please! I don't like to talk business at the table."

"Why not? I talk business morning, noon, and night," Rupert offered enthusiastically. "If I were like you, I'd still be selling cars in Cincinnati."

Nancy watched Brian's hands roll over into

fists. His voice was tense. "Rupert, give it a rest, huh?"

Kristin slid her fingertips along Brian's sleeve. "Darling, let's be sociable—"

Looking exasperated, Bree's father drew his arm away. "For pete's sake, Krissy—"

Kristin made a petulant face. "Brian, if your daughter's friend irritated you, that's no reason to snap at *me.*"

Nancy was startled by the spoiled resentment now darkening the actress's face. Kristin's clenched teeth looked ready to snip barbed wire.

"Cover your ears, Bree," she snapped. "Your father and I are about to have a spat."

Too late, Brian tried to make amends. He reached for Kristin's hand. "Now, honey—"

"Excuse me!" Kristin crumpled her napkin and threw it on the table. "I have a splitting headache. I'm going to bed. You may let yourselves out."

Head high, Kristin marched out of the room, slamming the louvered doors behind her. Making a weary sound, Brian left the table and wandered out to the patio. Rupert followed.

Bree looked acutely embarrassed. "And so ends another fun day in the life of the Gordon family. I'm really sorry, Nancy." She lifted her coffee cup in an ironic salute. "And to think people actually wonder why I don't want to get into the movies."

Nancy said nothing but felt a twinge of sympathy for Bree. The Gordon family was far from happy. Nancy couldn't help wondering about the underlying source of the tension.

Early the next morning Nancy and Bree set out again, this time to visit Tayo's sister. They left the car at the edge of a field of wind-tossed sugarcane, then hiked the narrow trail up the south slope of Orohena.

Nancy's cropped striped T-shirt and loose white knit shorts made for comfortable hiking. Ignoring the hum of insects near her ears, she stepped over huge feathery ferns and ducked beneath sodden, thorn-tipped vines.

The jungle thinned out, revealing a village of old-fashioned bamboo bungalows with thatched roofs. A cockatoo heckled them noisily. Shy piglets fled squealing at their approach.

Bree's mastery of Tahitian got them directions to Opane's house. Tayo's sister was in the yard, tilling her garden. She was a heavyset woman in her forties, wearing a brick red wraparound dress called a *pareo*. A huge white gardenia blossom nestled in her ink-black hair.

Opane's French was good. "What can I do for you?"

"If you don't mind," Nancy replied, "we'd like to ask you a few questions about your brother."

She glanced at them suspiciously. "You knew Tayo?"

"He worked aboard my family's yacht, the *Southwind*," Bree answered.

Opane blinked. "You're the movie woman!"

"No, I'm her daughter. Brée Gordon."

"Brée . . ." Opane's lips twitched. Then she smiled all over. Tugging at Bree's arm, she led the girls into her house. "He *said* you would come and you did!"

Nancy's eyes widened in surprise. "Let me get this straight. *Tayo* said Bree would come?"

"Yes. Years ago." She ushered them into the kitchen. "I have something for you, Bree."

Opane rummaged in the overhead cupboard. Then, with a triumphant grin, she withdrew a dusty cardboard box tied with string.

"Tayo was here just before he died," Opane explained, reaching for a paring knife. "He told me to keep this safe and give it to Bree."

Nancy bit the corner of her lower lip. Her hunch that Tayo had known he was in trouble seemed about to be proven correct.

Opane handed Bree the knife. The girl hesitated before the box, holding the blade awkwardly. "What is it?"

Opane lifted heavy shoulders in a shrug. "Don't ask me. Tayo was adamant. No one but Bree Gordon was to open it." Her hands shepherded Bree forward. "Go ahead, *chérie.*"

Bree's blade descended toward the string.

An eerie shiver rippled through Nancy. For four long years that box had been sitting on Opane's shelf, awaiting Bree.

A present from a dead man!

Chapter
Five

Snip! The keen edge cut the string.

Lifting the cardboard lid, Bree uttered a startled gasp.

Two objects lay at the bottom of the box. A barnacled steel anchor with a T-frame and sharp parallel flukes, and a slender, weed-encrusted chain.

Impaled on the fluke was a note in bold handwriting.

Nancy looked at Bree. "May I?"

Bree nodded, reaching into the box for the anchor. Bewilderment flooded her face.

Nancy hastily read the note.

Bree,

If you're reading this, then it's because I'm dead and could not show you the chain myself.

This is the *Southwind*'s anchor chain. Guard it well, Bree, for it is proof that your mother was murdered. I never believed the maritime board when they said the chain broke.

So last year I began diving at the *Southwind*'s old anchorage. I tried to avoid arousing suspicion, but it appears that I wasn't careful enough. Someone ransacked my boat yesterday. I think they were looking for this chain. I know it will be safe with Opane until you can use it to find the one who killed your mother.

I think maybe your mother's murderer is coming after me. If so, he's going to learn that old Tayo doesn't die so easy!

Take care of yourself, child.

Love,
Tayo

Nancy was conscious of a presence at her shoulder. Turning, she looked into Bree's stricken face. The black-haired girl shook her head in disbelief.

"It *can't* be true." Bree's eyes filled with tears. "Mother was *murdered!* It's not possible— I— oh, no!"

Bree broke down completely. Murmuring

words of comfort, Nancy and Opane helped her to the bedroom.

While Bree wept into a pillow, Nancy excused herself and returned to the kitchen. She ran the slender chain through her fingers. She was holding the first solid clue of the case. Now she just had to read it carefully.

Dried seaweed clung to the chain links. Nancy hefted the anchor. One end of the chain was firmly bolted to the anchor's shank. Bone-dry kelp filled the keyhole. Obviously, no one had tampered with that end since the day the anchor had first tasted salt water.

The other end told a different story. The final link had been cleanly severed. Nancy turned the sheared end toward the window and caught her breath. Sunshine gleamed on two long, straight gashes.

Somebody had used a hacksaw on this chain. Tayo was right. The *Southwind* didn't slip her anchor that night. She was deliberately cast adrift.

Opane entered the kitchen, her bare feet *slap-slapping* the bamboo floor. Her round face was solemn.

"I'll make us some tea," she said, moving to the woodstove.

Nancy replaced the anchor in the box. "Opane, when did Tayo give you this?"

The woman's face tensed thoughtfully. "It was the end of September. Four years ago." Tilting a bucket, she filled her brass teapot. "Tayo kept looking over his shoulder. He said, 'Opane, if anybody comes around asking for me, you haven't seen me for years. Understand?' Then he made me promise to give that box to Bree."

Nancy nodded. Tayo suspected that the killer was on to him. So he decided to hide his evidence in the safest place he could think of. He knew Opane would follow his instructions to the letter.

"One thing I don't understand," Nancy said, accepting a cup of tea. "Why did Tayo hide the evidence? Why didn't he take it to the police?"

Opane dumped sugar into her steaming cup, giving Nancy an embarrassed look. "He had good reason not to. Tayo was a wild one as a boy. When he was sixteen, he hijacked a rich man's boat to impress his girlfriend. He got caught and did three months at that prison camp in the Tuamotus. I think Tayo was afraid the police would blame *him* for the wreck."

Nodding, Nancy sipped her tea. She understood Tayo's fears. The police might not believe the story of a poor pearl diver with a previous record. No wonder Tayo had wanted Bree to present the evidence.

This also explained Tayo's strange preoccupation the last time Bree was in Tahiti. At that time, he was still trying to find proof of sabotage. He had found the chain at the end of September and had died a week or so later.

Nancy's skin prickled. Had Tayo Kapali been murdered?

It was more than possible. If so, the murderer

might still be loose on Tahiti—and someone like that would stop at nothing to ensure that the *Southwind* case remained closed!

On their way home Nancy and Bree stopped for a late lunch at Vaipahi waterfall. Tiny bright-colored birds fled, squawking noisily, as the two girls spread their picnic blanket on the lush grass.

"What do they call them?" Nancy asked, watching the tiny birds soar past the tumbling cascade.

"Huh?" Bree blinked, opening their picnic lunch. "Oh—those are vini birds. Scared little things. They take off at the first sight of people." With an apologetic look, she handed Nancy a sandwich. "Sorry. I'm not very good company today."

Nancy placed a sympathetic hand on the girl's shoulder. "Bree, are you going to be all right?"

"I-I— Oh, Nancy, I don't know if I can handle it." Bree sobbed, wiping away tears. "It's like Mother dying all over again."

Nancy offered her a soft drink. "Look, you don't have to talk about it if you don't want to."

"I *do* want to talk about it." Bree's eyes looked remote. "Mother was murdered. It's— Nancy, if I don't make sense of this, it's going to drive me crazy."

"Why don't you just start at the beginning?" Nancy advised soothingly. "Where were you when it happened?"

"At Faretaha. Krissy had invited us all to

spend the weekend, even Manda. She had a big party that Saturday night. Plenty of film people. I guess she wanted to show off the place. She'd just bought it with all the money she'd earned from *Horizon of Desire."* Bree steeled herself to go on. "I didn't stay at the party long. Just long enough to be polite."

Nancy nodded encouragement to continue and bit into her sandwich.

"I woke up in the middle of the night. The shutters were slamming," Bree continued. "I called for Manda. There was no answer. So I went downstairs. It was around two-fifteen—I remember looking at the clock. Everyone was gone. I figured Krissy must have moved the party downtown or something. The storm was getting pretty fierce. So I closed the shutters and headed back to bed."

"When did you hear about your mother?" Nancy asked, brushing crumbs from her lap.

"The next morning," Bree replied. "I was having breakfast on the terrace with Dad and Manda when a police car pulled into the drive. A lieutenant broke the news. I'll never forget the look on my father's face. He went white at first. Then he got this weird expression, as if he didn't know whether to be angry or sad. Manda just sat there, stunned."

Nancy could see that Bree was reliving that awful moment all over again.

"There was so much I didn't understand," Bree murmured, pressing her fingers to her temples. "Why had Mother gone back to the boat? I asked Dad, but he wouldn't talk about it. Every time I mentioned it, Dad put on that steely-eyed expression of his and changed the subject. So I eventually got the story out of Manda." Bree's voice began to break. "It's not pretty, Nancy. My parents had a big fight at the party. A typical Gordon battle. Loud and nasty. Mother slapped him, announced that she was sleeping aboard the *Southwind,* and stormed out."

"Bree, you said your mother *announced* her departure for the marina," Nancy observed.

The girl nodded.

"And she wasn't expected back that night," Nancy added.

"No, we were supposed to stay at Faretaha all weekend," Bree replied. "Nancy, what are you getting at?"

"Just this. No one knew beforehand that your mother would be aboard the *Southwind.* So, the murderer could not have cut the chain before the party. He or she must have been at Kristin's and heard your mother announce that she was leaving. Then the killer followed her back to the yacht."

Before Bree could reply, a screech filled the air. Nancy's gaze darted to the jungle. A flock of vini birds erupted from the treeline, cartwheeling into the sky.

Bree's words echoed in Nancy's brain. "Scared little things. They take off at the first sight of people."

Nancy's gaze dropped into the jungle and its thick moist vines, bamboo thickets, and moss-covered trees.

There's somebody in there! she thought. Somebody who spooked the birds.

Bree eyed her strangely. "Nancy, what is it?"

Just then, Nancy spied a glimmer of sunlight on a metal object. Her gaze zeroed in. A wickedly barbed spearpoint emerged from the foliage.

Shoom! The spear hurtled out of the jungle, speeding straight toward Bree!

Chapter

Six

"Look out!" Nancy cried.

She threw herself against Bree's chest. Both girls went sprawling. A whizzing sound cut the air. Stinging pain kissed Nancy's right shoulder.

Thunk! The spear buried itself in a palm trunk, quivering like a tuning fork.

"This way, Bree—*fast!*"

Nancy hauled the girl to her feet and shoved her into a thicket of tall ferns. Together they dropped behind an ancient lava flow.

Bree gasped. "You're hurt!"

Nancy glanced at her shoulder. The spear point had torn the sleeve of her T-shirt, its razor-edged fluke cleaving her skin. The shallow cut turned crimson. Nancy shuddered. Three inches lower, and that spear would have gone through the middle of her back!

"Just a scratch—I'll be okay," Nancy whispered, turning a fern aside. "Stay under cover, Bree. We don't want to give him a target."

Nancy scrutinized the wall of jungle carefully, but all was still. "No sign of anyone. But don't show your face just yet. He could be reloading."

For long, anxious moments, Nancy and Bree crouched behind the lava bed, waiting for the sniper to make his move. Then finally Nancy heard the start-up roar of a car engine. She ran to the edge of the clearing. Snapping noises behind the jungle's green façade announced the sniper's escape.

Nancy clamped her hand over her wound. "He's getting away!" Determined, she dashed across the clearing and plunged into the foliage.

She caught a glimpse of a small blue car fishtailing down a muddy pathway. The vehicle burst through a wall of greenery and, tires squealing, zoomed onto the main road.

Nancy scowled. The high ferns had hidden the license plate.

Bree came up behind her. "Nancy, you'd better treat that cut," she advised, pointing at the bloody sleeve. "Wounds get infected fast here in the tropics."

"I've got a first-aid kit in my car. Come on."

After bandaging Nancy's cut, the two girls returned to the picnic spot. Nancy went straight to the coconut palm and studied the spear.

"That's a—" Bree began to explain.

"A spear gun shaft. I know," Nancy replied, thinking back to her San Diego adventure, *Sisters in Crime.* "I have a friend who's a diver."

"I'm a diver myself," said Bree. "If you're going to commit murder, a spear gun's the perfect weapon. It's silent, and the carbon dioxide charge can drive a spearhead right through an oak board."

"That's for sure!" Nancy held out her hand. "Would you hand me one of the napkins?"

"What for?"

"I don't want to smudge any fingerprints that may be on the shaft," Nancy explained. "Then we'll see what other clues we can find."

A search of the surrounding jungle unearthed the sniper's hidden position. Pushing aside a thorn-laden branch, Nancy spotted a cluster of broken vines. Drawing closer, she spied the ferns mashed underfoot and the forest debris kicked up by the sniper's hasty retreat.

"Our friend took off like a deer," Nancy remarked, following the footprints deeper into the jungle. "Looks as if he or she didn't want you to catch a glimpse of— Whoa!"

Nancy halted on the muddy trail. Clearly outlined in the ooze was a diamond-shaped tread—a footprint identical to the one she had seen in Ruau's scrap yard.

Kneeling beside it, Nancy studied the print. The toes had dug in deep, but the arch and heel had skidded off to the right. She looked ahead.

The line of hasty footprints ended at a deep automobile tire mark.

It looks as if the sniper skidded on the mud while running to his car, she mused.

"Did you find anything?" asked Bree.

"Boat shoes." Nancy rose to her feet again. "I saw prints just like them at Ruau's, right after someone tried to drop a load of scrap on me. I'm pretty sure it's the same person." She sighed. It wasn't even sundown yet and she felt more than a little tired. "Let's get back to Papeete."

As they drove back to the city, Bree said, "It feels strange, you know? Except for you, I'm the only one who knows Mother was murdered. And I don't *dare* tell my father."

"Why not?" Nancy inquired.

"It's obvious, isn't it? The killer was at the party that night." Bree's eyes narrowed and she set her jaw. "She left right after Mother and followed her back to the boat."

"She?" Nancy echoed, glancing at her companion. "Bree, are you saying Kristin—"

"I don't know!" Thumping the dashboard, Bree groaned in misery. "Oh, what a *mess!*"

"Tell me why you think it might have been Kristin Stromm," Nancy suggested.

Leaning back in the passenger seat, Bree closed her eyes. "It was years ago—back in Hollywood. Krissy had just come over from Stockholm. Mother was a big star then. And— Well, to tell the truth, she wasn't exactly nice to newcomers. Krissy flubbed a take. Mother made a big thing of

47

it. Krissy said something catty. Next thing you know, it's World War Three on the soundstage." She looked somberly at Nancy. "It got even worse. Mother called her 'the Swedish Meatball' in a TV interview. Krissy lost a couple of big parts afterward. She was convinced Mother was deliberately trying to ruin her career."

Nancy took in this information impassively, but a question had been forming in her mind and now was the time to ask. "How do *you* feel about Kristin Stromm, Bree?"

"Well . . . it's hard to say. I don't dislike her—except when she treats me like a little kid. But we're not exactly buddy-buddy. Frankly, I think Krissy's—well, *shallow."* Bree looked highly uncomfortable. "I try to be nice to her. I tell myself, time and again, that I've got to accept it. I know Dad loves her. Still . . ." She bit her lower lip. "Oh, sometimes I wish Dad had found somebody else."

Nancy's mind was clicking away. Bree's answer satisfied her. If Bree had been trying to pin the blame on Kristin unfairly, she would have told Nancy that everything was wonderful.

No, Bree obviously had mixed feelings about her future stepmother. She didn't feel that Kristin was right for her father. And Bree felt guilty about that.

Nancy felt sorry for the girl whose life had seen such upheaval. She wondered if Brian Gordon was aware of his daughter's emotional turmoil.

Her thoughts turned back to the case. So

Lucinda Prado's fiery temper had caused her to make an enemy of Kristin Stromm. But had Kristin hated Lucinda enough to kill her?

Nancy nosed the Renault into the stream of rush-hour traffic in the city. The car crept along the Boulevard Pomare, serenaded by loud car horns.

With a sigh of relief, Nancy pulled into the Hotel Taravao's parking lot. "A traffic jam in Tahiti!" She got out of the car and grinned. "Even in paradise!"

Opening the car's trunk, she removed the spear gun shaft and the box containing Tayo's evidence. She wrapped the spear in a beach towel so it wouldn't attract attention. "One more question, Bree, before I get this evidence locked up. Did you tell anyone where we were going this morning?"

"Yes. I had breakfast with Dad and Krissy. She came over early this morning to see Dad and make up for their fight last night. I told them I was going to Orohena."

Nancy shut the trunk lid. "Were they the only people you told?"

"Yes. Oops, no, wait a minute!" Bree tapped her temple, as if to jog her memory. "Rupert stopped by just about then. He always comes by the hotel and mooches breakfast if he can. Oh, yes, and Manda had some vouchers for Dad to sign. She was there, too."

"Thanks, Bree."

Nancy watched as Bree pushed through the

glass doors into the lobby. In the last forty-eight hours the girl had learned of her mother's murder and the probable murder of an old friend. She was holding up pretty well under the strain, Nancy mused as she headed for the lobby.

A curly-haired Tahitian manned the front desk.

"May I help you, mademoiselle?"

"I'd like to store these overnight in the security vault." Nancy pushed the box and spear across the polished desktop.

The clerk had Nancy fill out a claim check. As Nancy watched him carry the items into the manager's office, she felt a small prick of guilt at not sharing all her suspicions with Bree. Obviously, someone had followed them from Opane's village to the waterfall. But how had he known that they would be at the village in the first place?

There were two possibilities, Nancy decided. Either their pursuer had been out on the highway, watching for Nancy's maroon Renault, or else he or she had overheard Bree telling her father about the trip.

When the clerk returned, Nancy thanked him. Then she realized he might be of more help. "Have you worked here long?" she asked politely.

"Ten years, mademoiselle."

"I guess you know the Gordons pretty well."

Teeth gleamed as he smiled. "Very well, indeed. I remember when Mademoiselle Bree was this high." His palm fluttered beside his waist.

Thinking fast, Nancy said, "We had a lovely drive today. It's a shame Ms. Stromm couldn't come with us."

The clerk blinked in surprise. "She didn't? Mademoiselle, she ran out of here right after you did."

Excitement made Nancy's pulse pound. "Really?"

"Yes." The clerk nodded. "Come to think of it, Madame Withers went out then, too."

Nancy blinked in surprise. "Oh," was all she said.

"Yes. Madame Withers asked me to phone a cab. After that I saw that other fellow—"

"Monsieur Holmberg," Nancy guessed.

"Yes, that's him. I saw him waiting rather impatiently at the bus stop just in front—here," he said, pointing.

"What about Bree's father?" Nancy asked.

"The monsieur I did not see leave," the clerk said matter-of-factly. "He phoned the desk to tell me he didn't want to be disturbed. Strange . . ."

"What's strange?" Nancy asked quickly.

"The cleaning woman said she saw Monsieur Gordon from the sundeck. He was walking down the beach toward the center of town."

"Have any of them returned?"

"I could not say, mademoiselle."

Nancy knew she had taken the interrogation as far as she could without making him suspicious. Thanking him for his help, she picked up her claims receipt and strolled away.

Nancy's mouth was a straight line as she thought, and her blue eyes were troubled. She didn't like the way the facts were adding up. Bree had told all four of them that she was driving down south to visit Opane. Within minutes of Bree's departure, all four had abruptly left the hotel.

Then someone had tried to kill Bree at Vaipahi waterfall. Coincidence?

Nancy couldn't help remembering that the same four people had disappeared from Faretaha the night Lucinda Prado had been murdered.

Kristin Stromm—Rupert Holmberg—Amanda Withers. Was one of them a murderer?

A queasy surge chilled Nancy as she focused on the fourth suspect—Bree's own father!

Chapter

Seven

THE NEXT AFTERNOON Nancy brought her evidence to the gendarmerie. A policeman escorted her to the detective bureau.

Captain Tuana Mutoi, the chief of detectives, was a tall, good-looking man in his early thirties, with curly, jet black hair, deep-set eyes, and a firm chin. Nancy was struck by how dashing he looked in his khaki uniform and white cap.

Mutoi listened politely as Nancy told her story. His eyes dispassionately studied the spear and the severed anchor chain.

"That's where we stand right now," Nancy concluded, smoothing her cotton skirt. "The way I see it, whoever killed Lucinda Prado and Tayo

Kapali is still here on the island. He or she got nervous when Bree started looking for Tayo. That's when the murder attempts began."

"Are you asking for protection for yourself and Mademoiselle Gordon?" Captain Mutoi asked, folding his hands on the blotter.

"Not exactly," Nancy replied. "I was hoping we could work together on this. Maybe smoke him out."

The captain smiled indulgently. "Mademoiselle Drew, I think you'd better leave police work to the professionals."

Nancy had heard words like those enough times before to know that she shouldn't let her frustration show. Instead she gave him an engaging smile and replied evenly, "Captain, I have helped police departments in the States on many occasions—"

"I'm sure you have," he interrupted smoothly, putting the anchor chain back in its box. "And I thank you for bringing this matter to my attention." Skepticism laced his words as he reached for the spear gun shaft. "I'll have the lab dust this for fingerprints."

Nancy's heart sank. From his tone of voice, she could tell that any such test would have an extremely low priority.

Captain Mutoi leaned back in his chair. "Is there anything else we can do for you?"

Nancy chose her words carefully. "Maybe there is. Would you mind if I had a look at the original *Southwind* accident report?"

"What for?"

"Bree's told me so much about it," Nancy added, hoping her alibi sounded plausible. "I'm curious."

"I can't see any harm in that." Leaning forward the captain wrote Nancy a permission slip. "There! You'll find the archives upstairs. Oh, and if you come across anything else like this"—he tapped his pen on the spear-gun shaft—"by all means, let me have a look."

After thanking Captain Mutoi, Nancy went upstairs. The archives clerk handed her a thick volume and pointed out an empty desk at the far end of the room.

Nancy spent the next few hours reading the report of the inquest. She covered everything, from Tahiti's weather that day to a description of the collision to Lucinda Prado's autopsy. On her notepad, Nancy jotted down the names of witnesses who had appeared at the inquest.

When she was finished, Nancy returned the book and went downstairs to the maritime office. Most of the witnesses had been boat owners anchored near the *Southwind*. It was a long shot, but Nancy wanted to see if any of them were still in Tahiti.

She was in luck. Of the eight boat owners who originally gave testimony, two were still listed as residents by the maritime office. Nancy hurriedly copied their current addresses. Then, after thanking the clerk, she strolled out of the office.

As she walked past the detective bureau, she

heard a pair of masculine voices, one of them Captain Mutoi's. Their words caught her attention, and she halted for a moment to listen.

"What have you got on the smugglers, Lucien?"

"My informers tell me there's a new shipment of computer parts in town, sir. Very expensive goods, I hear. Prototypes of Japan's newest hardware—system cards, mostly, with multi-megabyte memory capacity. The word is that they're soon to be shipped to South America."

Frustration deepened the captain's voice. "Who, Lucien? Who's behind this?"

"No one knows, sir. They're well organized—and well hidden!"

"Put everyone on it. Double-check every ship leaving Papeete," Captain Mutoi ordered. "This gang has been plundering Japanese computer factories for years. The Japanese police traced them here to Tahiti. Both Japan and our government want us to put them out of business—for good!"

Looks as if Bree and I are on our own, Nancy thought, striding into the parking lot. The Tahitian police have their hands full with those computer smugglers.

Minutes later Nancy was strolling along Charterboat Row, the section of waterfront devoted to sports fishing. Sleek cabin cruisers bobbed in the gentle swell, sunlight flashing on their chrome fittings.

She spied the name *Galilee* on the stern of a

sturdy Gulfstar 36. A wiry, brown-skinned man in a Greek skipper's cap stood on her foredeck, expertly winding a line around a cleat.

Cupping her hands to her mouth, Nancy cried, "Ahoy, the *Galilee!*"

"*Bonjour,* there." The man's U.S. accent fractured the French words.

Nancy switched to English. "Hi, I'm looking for Josh Tuttle."

"You found him."

"My name's Nancy Drew. I'm a friend of Bree Gordon's. I'd like to ask you a few questions about the *Southwind.* Do you mind?"

"Not at all." He walked around the deck and put down the gangway for Nancy. "Welcome aboard! How is young Bree, by the way?"

"Pretty good. She's going to UCLA these days." Nancy followed him into the boat's screened cabin. He gestured to a settee, and she took a seat. "Did you know the Gordons very well?"

Tuttle grinned. "Well enough. There are no secrets in boat basins. I liked them. No movie-star airs on that Lucinda. When she was out here on vacation, she was plain old Mrs. Gordon, and that's the way she liked it."

"How did Brian Gordon strike you?" Nancy asked."

"Money-hungry—" Tuttle broke off quickly and narrowed his eyes. "You ask a lot of questions, Ms. Drew. How come?"

"Some disturbing questions have come up

about the wreck of the *Southwind*. Bree asked me to check them out." Nancy settled back in the cushions. "Would you mind telling me about the accident?"

"Sure! I'm used to it by now. Why, I'm practically the boat basin's official *Southwind* historian." Now Tuttle seemed to enjoy peering into the past. "I'd just gotten back from a day trip. Found a snug anchorage near the lee shore and put down a pair of anchors."

"It seems I've found an expert sailor," Nancy commented.

"Been at it twenty years." Tuttle grinned self-consciously, then took a quick breath. "Anyway, the night Lucinda died, there was a big storm. It kicked up quite a chop. I could feel the surge tugging at *Galilee*'s hull.

"At about two A.M. I heard a motor and thought, 'What fool's out on a night like this?' I went topside, just in time to see Lucinda go by in a dinghy headed for *Southwind*. Thought she'd capsize in the swell, but she just rode the current all the way and climbed on board *Southwind*. Quite a sailor, that woman!

"Anyway, I went below, then I remembered that I'd left my deck lights on. So I went topside again. And *Southwind* was gone now! All I saw was one moored boat and the channel buoy. It sure was rough water out there! The buoy's bell was ringing, and its little green light was swinging back and forth. I doused my deck lights and hit the sack."

"When did you hear about the wreck?"

"Next morning. It was all over Papeete."

Nancy mulled over his story. Tuttle had seen Lucinda board the *Southwind* at 2:00 A.M. When he went topside again at 2:30, the vessel was gone. That matched the times in the official report.

Standing, Nancy gave him a grateful smile. "Thanks for taking time to talk to me, Mr. Tuttle."

"Any friend of Bree's is a friend of mine." He slid the screen door open for Nancy. "You tell her I said hi."

"I will," Nancy promised, halting at the gangway. "Oh, one more thing—you wouldn't know where I might be able to find Pierre Panchaud, would you? I didn't see his name on file at the maritime office."

Genuine surprise washed over his face. "That's strange! Talk around town is that Pierre's got his own boat."

"I didn't see it listed," Nancy replied.

"Maybe you're right." Tuttle shrugged. "I haven't seen Pierre working *these* waters, and I'm out every day. Try the Café Chat Noir ashore. I hear Pierre hangs out down there."

"Café Chat Noir." Nancy committed the name to memory. "Where do I find it?"

"Rue des Écoles." He tilted his head eastward. "But you be careful down there, Ms. Drew. That is one rough neighborhood!"

* * *

The Café Chat Noir stood on a narrow side street, flanked by a couple of taverns. Its checkerboard awning had seen better days. The silhouette of a huge black cat, outlined in neon, perched on top of a weather-beaten cinema marquee.

Clutching her shoulder bag, Nancy walked inside, out of the early-evening dusk. An old-fashioned ceiling fan twirled lazily. An empty stage, its curtains down, marked the far end of the restaurant.

Nancy was suddenly aware of a presence at her side. She turned at once.

The maître d' eyed her coolly. He reminded Nancy of the fat man in the old movie *The Maltese Falcon.*

"A table, mademoiselle?"

"Actually," Nancy said, "I'm looking for a man named Panchaud. Pierre Panchaud. Have you seen him around?"

His lips tightened. "Now and then."

"Do you know where I might find him?"

The maître d' turned his palms upward in a gesture of ignorance.

"How about Pierre's friends?" Nancy persisted.

"You might talk to them." Looking a bit smug, he pointed to a pair of rough-looking French sailors seated at a table near the stage. "New boys in town, but Pierre finds them friendly enough."

"Thank you." Nancy manufactured a bright smile, then headed across the room.

The men stood as Nancy approached their

table. One was thin-faced and swarthy, with buck teeth. The other was taller, built like a linebacker, wearing a striped shirt and a black beret.

"Excuse me," Nancy said. "Could you tell me where to find Pierre Panchaud?"

Thin Face sneered at her. "Get lost!"

Nancy tried her most winning smile. "Look, I just want to ask him a few questions about—"

Black Beret grabbed a tall wine bottle from the table. In one quick move he smashed it against the chair. Brandishing the bottleneck like a knife, he aimed the razor-sharp fragment at Nancy's face!

Chapter

Eight

THE JAGGED BOTTLE EDGE rushed toward her. Heart hammering, Nancy threw herself sideways to avoid the thrust, and at the same moment grabbed the Frenchman's wrist and turned it aside. Then, stepping in close, she smashed her right elbow into the thug's bicep.

Black Beret shrieked in pain. His nerveless fingers dropped the broken bottle. It shattered on the floor.

Thin Face rushed her. "You little—!"

Bracing herself against the table, Nancy launched a scissor kick at the newcomer. Her sole struck the sailor flush on the jaw, knocking him sprawling.

Suddenly a deafening electric bell rang out. Nancy looked up just in time to see the maître d' lift his hand from a countertop button.

A voice hollered, "It's a raid!" A rear door burst open. Dozens of panicky, well-dressed people rushed into the room. Brushing her hair out of her face, Nancy stared in confusion.

Then she caught a glimpse of a stunning blonde in a shimmery emerald evening gown, eyes wide with alarm, sprinting away on her stiletto heels.

Nancy blinked in recognition. Kristin Stromm! What was she doing there?

Nancy heard footsteps running behind her. Turning, she saw her two erstwhile opponents scramble for the front door. Although she was tempted to give chase, she decided to let them go. She was more interested in what Kristin was doing here.

A quick peek through the open doorway provided the answer. A roulette wheel crowned one long table. The others were covered with green felt and white dice.

The maître d' waddled past Nancy and closed the door. "Now that you've chased all my customers away, would you kindly leave?"

Nancy folded her arms. "Gambling's illegal in French Polynesia, isn't it?"

The maître d' tossed her a defiant look. "You didn't actually *see* anyone gambling, did you?"

No, thought Nancy, but I saw you hit the alarm

button. And I doubt Kristin Stromm comes here for the cuisine.

"Goodbye, mademoiselle." His pudgy finger pointed at the front door. "If you really are looking for Pierre Panchaud, I understand he owns a dive shop on the Rue des Halles."

"Why didn't you tell me that before?" Nancy asked, thoroughly annoyed.

The maître d' shrugged indifferently. "I didn't know you were an agent of the Deuxième Bureau before."

Nancy understood at once, and she couldn't suppress a grin. The Deuxième Bureau was the French FBI. Seeing her karate performance, the maître d' must have thought she was an undercover cop and had hit the alarm button.

Smoothing her skirt, Nancy walked out of the café. She couldn't shake the image of the fleeing actress. So Kristin liked to gamble. Nancy wondered what to make of that fact—and if Bree or Brian Gordon knew about it.

Nancy pursed her lips thoughtfully. It was certainly interesting, that Kristin should frequent the favorite café of Pierre Panchaud, the *Southwind*'s sole survivor.

She would look up Pierre as soon as she finished interviewing the other *Southwind* witnesses. She had a few questions for that man.

Later that evening Nancy stepped out of her hotel bathroom, vigorously toweling her damp hair. She was looking forward to relaxing, reading a magazine, and reviewing her notes on the perplexing case. Just then the telephone jangled. Dropping the towel, she tied the belt of her terry-cloth robe and hurried over to the night table.

Picking up the receiver, she heard a male voice say thickly, "Eez thees ze most bee-ootiful girl in Tahiti?"

Nancy was stumped for a moment. Then she caught on. "Ned, that was awful!" she said, laughing.

"Nancy! I can't fool you, can I?" Ned's laughter joined hers on the line. "How are you?"

"Fine!" The sound of her boyfriend's voice was sending a happy tingle through Nancy's nerves. "How are you doing?"

"Tearing my hair out over a term paper. It's half the grade for the course. But I'd rather hear about your case." His curiosity was noticeable even over the wires.

"It's taken a strange turn, Ned."

Nancy quickly filled him in on the events of the past few days. When she was finished, he let out a low whistle.

"A five-year-old murder! You sure know how to pick them, Nancy. You really think it was one of Lucinda Prado's inner circle?"

"It sure looks that way. Lucinda and her family left the *Southwind* on Friday night. Kristin's big party was Saturday night. I read the witnesses' statements. Nobody at the anchorage expected Lucinda back until Monday."

"So the only people who knew she was aboard the yacht were the people at Kristin's party," Ned added. "Who's your number-one suspect?"

"It's too soon to guess, Ned," she replied, holding the phone in her lap. "I still wonder why the house was empty when Bree woke up. And where was Manda? She was an overnight guest there too. Where was Bree's father?"

"Good questions!" Ned's voice sounded troubled. "Listen, if you need me, say so. I can hop a plane and be in Tahiti in twenty-four hours."

"Thanks, Ned, I appreciate that. But I can handle myself. I'll be fine."

"I hope so. You're my precious, irreplaceable Nancy Drew. I do worry about you. Especially when there are nut cases running around with broken bottles!"

A warm feeling rushed through Nancy. With a smile, she murmured, "I'll be extra careful on this one, Ned." She blew a kiss into the phone. "I love you, Nickerson!"

"Love you, too, Drew. Take care!"

Slowly, regretfully, Nancy replaced the receiver. She wondered if she had made a mistake in turning down Ned's offer of help. There was a killer out there, a shrewd enemy who seemed to want only one thing: Nancy Drew and Bree Gordon—dead!

* * *

The following morning Nancy met Bree in the Taravao's broad lobby. They had made plans to visit another witness, Alistair Pendleton, an Englishman who had seen Lucinda on the night of the accident. Bree looked tired and drawn. She put her hands in the pockets of her short denim skirt, her dark eyes mournful. Nancy decided she would try to keep Bree's mind off her mother as much as possible.

As they walked out to the car, Nancy asked, "Bree, has Kristin ever mentioned a café called the Chat Noir?"

"Not that I know of." Bree's eyebrows arched with curiosity. "Why do you ask?"

Nancy opened her car door. "I saw her there last night, gambling in the back room."

Bree made a pinched face. "Oh, brother! Dad will be furious. After the last time, Krissy swore she'd never do it again."

Nancy pushed open the passenger door from the inside. "What happened the last time?"

"Dad and Krissy went to Vegas last year," Bree explained. "Krissy went a little crazy at the tables. Dad covered her losses. They were still arguing when they got home."

Nancy needed no further information to imagine the battle.

"If you don't mind a personal question," she began, "did your parents ever fight about money?"

Bree was silent, obviously reliving the past.

"Money was never an issue that I knew of. Not like Mother wanting to quit the film industry. She was determined to retire to Tahiti—and soon. It made for some rousing battles, believe me."

Sensing the girl's distress, Nancy fell silent. She remembered Tuttle's comment. He'd thought that Brian was very interested in money, probably his wife's. However, now, according to Bree, that wasn't the case at all. Nancy herself had gotten the impression that money wasn't all that important to Brian.

Which left only one other motive for him to kill his wife—Kristin Stromm.

With his marriage in trouble, had Brian been attracted to the beautiful Swedish actress? Nancy left the speculation dangling for the moment.

As they drove through Pendleton's neighborhood of Pamatai, Nancy admired the fine old bungalows built on a ridge overlooking a sparkling turquoise bay.

Alistair Pendleton answered the doorbell, finally embracing Bree when his failing eyesight confirmed who she was—the daughter of his old friend. He invited the girls inside. Bree offered to prepare some lemonade in the kitchen while Nancy and Pendleton retired to the drawing room.

"Oh, I'll never forget that night." Leaning back in a plush chair, Pendleton lit his meerschaum pipe. "I was staying on my boat then, and the rough sea kept me awake. Precisely at two A.M. I heard a motor. Looking out the porthole, I saw Lucinda go past in a dinghy. I watched her until she climbed aboard the *Southwind,* just to make certain she was safe, you understand." He took a long pull on his pipe. "Shortly thereafter, I became a bit queasy."

"So you went topside," Nancy prodded.

"Quite." Brows tensing, he chewed the pipe-stem. "The bell buoy was bobbing like a cork in a millrace, green light swinging. I saw the Moorea ferry on her way in, the waves smashing her bow. Oh, yes, and there was that woman."

"What woman?" Nancy asked, her eyes narrowing with interest.

"On the beach. Dark-haired, wearing a trench coat. She was walking up and down. Quite anxious, if you ask me. I assume she was looking for a boat, you know. But I didn't see any, and neither did she." He tapped the pipe against a small ashtray. "She didn't linger. Once or twice, she seemed to look at the *Southwind,* as if trying to come to a decision. Then she drew up her collar and hurried away. Odd, eh?"

"I'll say." Nancy filed away this bit of news. "When did you notice that the *Southwind* was missing?" she inquired.

"At two-thirty, I believe. Yes. I looked out the porthole again. *Southwind* was gone. Lucinda was a smashing sailor, but not even she would have gone out in that storm."

"Had you been surprised to see Lucinda back aboard the yacht?" Nancy asked.

A frown on his lips, Pendleton glanced quickly at the kitchen. Turning to Nancy again, he deliberately lowered his voice.

"I do hope you'll keep this to yourself, Nancy. Bree's a lovely girl, and I know it would only upset her." He lit his pipe again. "I wasn't at all surprised to see Lucinda. She and Brian had had the most dreadful quarrel on deck that afternoon." His face puckered in distaste. "I do wish couples wouldn't fight in public."

That was one story Nancy fully intended to keep to herself. "Mr. Pendleton, would you say the Gordons' marriage had just about had it?"

"Not really," Pendleton replied, after a moment's reflection. "For all his arrogance, Brian's a bit weak. He leaned on Lucinda. She was very proud, fiery, yet old-fashioned in her ideas about marriage. Oh, she talked divorce a lot. But that's all it was—just talk."

Nancy thought of Kristin Stromm. "Would Lucinda have divorced Brian if there was another woman in the picture?"

Pendleton frowned. "Divorce, no. Have a public row, yes."

"She was that jealous, huh?"

"Quite! Poor Brian would have had to scramble up the nearest palm tree."

"Thanks for your help, Mr. Pendleton," Nancy said, smiling in spite of her growing uneasiness about Bree's father.

Bree came in with two glasses and then, catching Nancy's eye, wandered out to the garden.

Nancy pressed on. "Tell me, is there anyone else in Tahiti I could talk to about Lucinda Prado?"

"Well, you could try Rupert Holmberg." The Englishman set aside his pipe. "He was always hanging about the *Southwind,* trying to get Lucinda to sign for one of his comedy films. In fact, he bought his own boat several years ago. Carbon copy of the *Southwind.* Rupert was very much impressed with Lucinda's yacht."

"How do you know that?" Nancy set down her glass. "Are you a friend of Rupert's?"

"Actually, it's more of a business relationship. He's not my sort of chap at all." Pendleton stood up. "Before my retirement I was employed by an insurance firm. Once in a great while I still write a policy. Two months before Lucinda's death Rupert asked me to write a three-million-dollar policy on her."

Nancy stiffened as the significance of the fact sank in. Pendleton caught the look on her face. "I thought the deal a bit dicey myself, but Rupert assured me that it was done all the time in Hollywood," he offered.

"Do you recall the precise terms of the policy?"

"Oh, yes. The coverage was not on Lucinda or her life expectancy, you understand. It was on something called forfeiture of assurance."

"What's that?" Nancy asked.

"Well, apparently Rupert and Lucinda had been discussing her participation in his new comedy film. Although no contract had been signed, Rupert felt that he had Lucinda's 'assurance' that she would star in it. In order to protect that 'assurance,' Rupert took out the policy. In the event that catastrophic illness or death prevented Lucinda from doing the film, Rupert would be able to collect compensatory payment."

To Nancy it sounded like a perfect scheme to swindle the insurance company. "And you're telling me a company *accepted* that policy?"

Looking highly uncomfortable, Pendleton replied, "Well, Rupert did pay cash, you know. A sixty-thousand-dollar premium. The bidding company thought it a marvelous investment. Lucinda was a healthy, vigorous woman of forty-two—they thought they would never have to pay it."

"Big surprise for them," Nancy added. "Do you have any idea why Rupert wanted that policy?"

"He refused to say, but there were rumors of severe money troubles," Pendleton reminisced. "Without Lucinda as the star of his next comedy film, he was certain to end in bankruptcy." He shook his head in amazement. "Protecting that 'assurance' was a most prudent move, as things turned out. That three million bailed Rupert out of financial trouble."

At that moment Bree came back in from the garden. "Am I missing something?"

"Nothing much. Mr. Pendleton has been a big help." Nancy exchanged a look of understanding with the Englishman as he opened the front door. "Thanks again."

"You're quite welcome, Nancy. Take care of yourself, Bree."

As they headed back to the Renault, Nancy pondered these new developments. What did Rupert have in mind when he took out that policy?

Bree had told her that Lucinda was determined to quit the film business. Rupert had desperately needed a Lucinda Prado movie to bail himself out of trouble. He would have gone broke but for that timely insurance policy.

Nancy turned grim. That policy put a whole new light on things. If Rupert had known of Lucinda's decision to retire, then he would have had the strongest motive for killing her—a three-million-dollar motive!

After a shoreside lunch Nancy and Bree visited the Rue des Halles, Tahiti's bustling open-air market. As they strolled along the sun-baked pavement, Nancy had to remind herself to ignore the colorful merchandise that spilled from the jumble of tiny shops. Her one aim now was finding the diving store that belonged to Pierre Panchaud.

A bell jangled as Nancy pushed the door open. A muscular, dark-haired man in his late twenties stood behind the counter, examining a pair of scuba tanks. He had a lean face, with a cleft chin and a pair of piercing hazel eyes.

Those eyes narrowed as the girls approached the counter. "Bree Gordon."

"Hi, Pierre. It's been awhile, I guess." Bree's smile was polite.

Setting aside the scuba gear, he asked, "What brings you downtown, mademoiselle?"

"We wanted to talk to you about the *Southwind,*" Bree said hopefully.

"I did all my talking to the maritime board. The *Southwind*'s ancient history." Pierre's expression turned decidedly unfriendly. "I've put the sea behind me."

Nancy spoke up. "That's not what I've heard."

"And who are you?" he asked dryly.

"My name's Nancy Drew. I'm a friend of Bree's."

"Then I don't need to answer *your* questions." His tone had turned frosty.

Keeping her voice polite, Nancy met his hostile gaze evenly. "Have you something to hide?"

"Nothing at all." Pierre drew himself erect. "I will tell you what you want to know about the *Southwind.*"

"How long had you known Bree's mother before she died?" Nancy inquired.

"Not long. I was in Japan five years ago, I needed a ride home to Tahiti and heard the *Southwind* was fitting out. So I signed on and sailed with her to Tahiti."

"Tell us about the storm."

"There's not much to tell. I had the all-night watch," Pierre said matter-of-factly. "The family

74

had already gone ashore in the dinghy. I took it back out to the boat and relieved Tayo. Then he went ashore in it. Around two A.M., Lucinda climbed up the stern ladder and startled me. I hadn't expected her back until Monday. She told me she was sleeping aboard, then went to her stateroom. That's the last I saw of her." His tone deepened. He seemed to be reliving the accident.

"The storm surge worsened. I went below to check out the pumps. On my way back I stopped in the galley for a bite to eat. The *Southwind* was really rolling with the swell. I could hear the buoy's bell ringing outside. I looked through one of the portholes and saw the buoy's green light and the big Moorea ferry passing astern."

He paused for a moment as Nancy waited expectantly. So far his story sounded no different from the other accounts she'd heard. He took a breath. "When the freighter rammed us, I ran up the companionway, yelling 'Abandon ship!' That boat went down like a brick! I barely had time to grab a life preserver and jump into the sea."

Nancy turned to Bree, concerned that the girl might be finding this hard to take, but her lips were set in a determined line. "Do you know Kristin Stromm?" Nancy pursued.

"By sight. She came aboard the *Southwind* once or twice. And I've seen her movies."

"Have you ever seen her at the Café Chat Noir?" asked Nancy, flashing him a speculative glance.

Pierre froze. His expression suddenly became

angry. "You're mistaken," he said stiffly. "I don't go there."

Nancy recalled what Josh Tuttle and the café's maître d' had told her. "People say they've seen you in there."

All at once, Pierre balled his fist. His enraged blow rattled the counter.

"I don't like being called a liar!" Furious, Pierre shook his fist at Nancy. "Do yourself a favor. Get out of here! If you mess with me, you're *really* going to get hurt!"

Chapter

Nine

Nancy was startled by the hostile gesture, but she stood her ground. "Is that a threat, Pierre?"

"Take it any way you like." He pointed firmly at the front door. "Just get out of here!"

Nancy knew she would get nothing more from Pierre. "Let's go, Bree." Taking her arm, Nancy led the girl out into the crowded street.

Bree trembled with suppressed anger. "He's a bum, Nancy. He always was." She stalked away angrily.

Nancy glanced back at the dive shop. Pierre Panchaud was no friend of the Gordons. As a diver he was certainly familiar with spear guns. But had he killed Lucinda? And, if so, what could his motive possibly have been?

"Where to next?" asked Bree as they headed back to the car.

"I thought we might have a look at the spot where the *Southwind* was anchored," Nancy replied. "Tayo found that chain. Perhaps there's another clue down there."

"Good idea." Bree nodded in agreement. "We can rent some scuba gear back at the hotel."

As they drove back to the Taravao, Nancy mulled over Pierre's story. The man was certainly unpleasant enough, but Nancy found it hard to think of him as a murderer. Pierre had never even met Lucinda before that summer.

The other suspects had genuinely compelling reasons to kill her. Kristin had hated Bree's mother. She had considered Lucinda her biggest screen rival.

Nancy reflected again on the obvious fact that Rupert stood to gain much-needed money. And for Brian, Lucinda's death had been the ticket out of a stormy marriage.

Nancy shook her head as she considered her most recent encounter. Pierre's story meshed perfectly with the reminiscences of the other *Southwind* witnesses. All reported the same things—the ferry passing astern, the green light on the buoy, the ringing bell.

Nancy frowned thoughtfully. So Pierre must have been belowdecks that night, just as he had said. The man's alibi seemed ironclad.

But why did Pierre lie about the Café Chat Noir? And why had those two Frenchmen attacked her after she had casually mentioned Pierre's name?

Nancy had to wonder if the two men were involved in Lucinda's murder. If so, how? They were definitely linked to Pierre Panchaud.

Nancy felt more than a little bewildered by so many possibilities and so little proof. But she was not about to give up. Things were just getting interesting.

After changing Nancy entered the Gordon penthouse suite. She found Amanda Withers on the sofa, prim as ever in a tailored apricot linen suit. She shuffled business papers, her steel-rimmed glasses low on her sharp nose. Nancy paused expectantly in the doorway.

Manda removed her glasses. "Hello, Nancy. Are you looking for Bree?"

"Yes. We're meeting here." Nancy took a chair across from the secretary. "She's renting some scuba tanks so we can have a look at the *Southwind*'s old anchorage."

"That again." With a sigh, Manda set her papers on the coffee table. "Sometimes I don't think we'll ever hear the end of it."

"I guess you've seen a lot working for the family all these years," Nancy commented.

"Indeed I have." Giving Nancy a conspiratorial smile, Manda leaned forward. "I could tell you stories. Of course, it's not my place to gossip. But if you knew the truth about *her . . . !*"

"Her?" Nancy echoed.

"Kristin Stromm." Manda spat out the name as if it were poison. "You know, the night Lucinda drowned, Kristin was nowhere to be found. She left her own party right after Brian and Lucinda quarreled. I wonder where she went. Don't you?"

I could ask the same question of you, Manda, thought Nancy. She ignored the secretary's insinuations, though, and changed the subject. "You don't sound very happy with your job."

"Oh! Don't get me wrong. I adore working for the family. Bree's a darling." Manda's gaze softened. "And Brian, he's such a wonderful man. Absolutely brilliant. A true cinema genius."

"How did you get along with Lucinda?" Nancy asked carefully.

"Fairly well, I suppose." Manda wrinkled her nose in distaste. "She was *such* a demanding woman. She bullied poor Brian unmercifully. Had the vilest temper I've ever seen. I'd have given my notice in a minute, if not for Brian." She tugged self-consciously at her skirt.

"Her death was quite a shock to him. He was so lonely. If only he could have met the right woman—someone kind, thoughtful, even-tempered, intellectual, loving . . .'"

Nancy struggled not to smile. She could guess who fit *that* description.

"Well, he does have Kristin," Nancy observed.

80

"It's a travesty," Manda snapped, tight-lipped with emotion. "Brian and that— *Ohhh!*" Eyes narrowing furiously, she added, "Kristin Stromm is a shallow, man-hungry fortune hunter! She's been chasing Brian for years. The night of the party Lucinda had to drag him away from her. If you ask me, that woman is completely unfit to be his wife!"

"Well, it's his choice," Nancy replied evenly.

Manda stood quickly, an angry blush coloring her heart-shaped face. "How can you be so complacent about it? Bree's your *friend*. Don't you care that her father's marrying that—that tramp?"

The passion in the secretary's voice startled Nancy. Clearly, hidden fires blazed within Amanda Withers.

Just as quickly a cool mask descended on her features. "If you'll excuse me, I have some business to attend to." Performing a quick about-face, Manda marched out of the living room, head high, heels punishing the hardwood floor.

Nancy watched her go, reflecting on the new factor that had been added to the equation. She felt bad for upsetting Manda, but the woman was clearly not very rational on the subject of the Gordon family.

It took no special skill to see that Manda was head-over-heels in love with Brian Gordon. Beneath her prim exterior seethed a savage jealousy. She now hated Kristin Stromm as ardently as she had once hated Lucinda Prado.

Nancy suddenly remembered something. Bree had told her that when she awakened at Faretaha, she had called for Manda. There had been no answer.

Questions flitted through Nancy's mind. Why did Manda leave the estate that night? Where did she go?

Suspicion provided some ugly answers. Manda was practically part of the Gordon family. She knew that Lucinda would never divorce her husband. What if she had taken advantage of the Gordons' quarrel that night?

Manda might have followed her employer back to the yacht. Indeed, she'd lived aboard the *Southwind* too. She knew all about the anchor chain.

How simple it would have been to cut the chain while Lucinda slept, to watch as the *Southwind* drifted toward certain destruction.

Manda's motive would have been simplicity itself. With Lucinda dead, Brian would have been free to marry her!

"Have you ever tried this before?" asked Bree, sliding a flipper onto her foot.

"Once or twice." Nancy smiled. "You may have to refresh me."

The girls were standing in the cockpit of a sleek twenty-foot runabout. Beside the boat, a red-and-white dive flag bobbed on its Styrofoam buoy.

Bree went through a run-down as she boosted a

tank rig onto Nancy's shoulders. "You'll be okay. Just remember to keep an eye on that air gauge."

Nancy buckled the support straps. "What about sharks?"

Bree tightened her weight belt. "Oh, forget all those movies. You rarely see sharks in the boat basin. Besides, they aren't *that* dangerous. They only go crazy if they smell blood. You leave them alone, they'll leave you alone."

Nancy studied the sun-dappled water. "Are you sure?"

"Positive." Bree grinned. "Sharks have their own body language. If you see a shark swimming in a tight circle, with his fins pointed straight down, that means he's angry and will attack."

Gooseflesh rippled along Nancy's bare arms. With a weak smile, she mounted the gunwale. "Thank you, Bree, for knowledge I never want to use!"

After putting the regulator in her mouth, Nancy backflipped into the sea.

Warm waters closed around her. Air bubbles drifted through her floating hair. Waving her arms languidly, Nancy looked around, startled and delighted by the beauty of the lagoon.

A school of bright red clownfish zigzagged through the turquoise water. Anemone strands soared upward from the coral reef, swaying in the mild current. A large sea turtle coasted along the bottom, making a wide detour around the girls.

Bree, in her lemon yellow maillot, performed a graceful jackknife turn and headed for the bottom. Nancy, in her emerald swimsuit, followed close behind.

Soon Bree and Nancy were cruising along the seabed, kicking in tandem, their air bubbles streaming to the surface. This is great, Nancy thought. I could stay down here forever—if I didn't have a mystery to solve!

Halting at a broad, level spot, Bree pantomimed a shipwreck. Nancy nodded in understanding. This was where the *Southwind* had anchored.

Together they searched the area. Nancy's fingertips probed the loose black sand.

She thought of Tayo. How many times had he swooped down to this very spot, searching for the clue he knew must be there?

Just then a shadow blotted out the sun. Looking up, Nancy saw a hull drifting overhead. Her brows knit in concern. Motorboats were forbidden to enter any area with a dive flag. What was the matter with that guy?

Keeping her eyes on the boat, Nancy swam closer to Bree.

A figure appeared at the transom. The hull rocked under its weight. Rippling water distorted the image. Nancy couldn't tell if it was male or female.

The figure lifted a slender object to its shoulder.

Nancy reacted instantly. Rolling in the water, she shoved Bree away with her flippered feet.

Whizzz! A spear gun shaft zipped past Bree, burying itself in the sand.

Nancy looked up. The shadowy figure was hurriedly reloading.

Nancy looked frantically around, seeking cover but finding none. For the killer, it would be like shooting fish in a barrel.

Nancy and Bree were trapped!

Chapter

Ten

Nancy watched helplessly as the sniper lifted the spear gun again.

Suddenly Bree tapped her shoulder. Whirling, Nancy saw the black-haired girl gripping her own weight belt. Her free hand tugged at Nancy's.

The emergency release!

Nancy pressed the tab with her palm. Instantly the weight belt slid past her thighs. Nancy left the bottom like an air bubble, Bree at her side, speeding to the surface. Remembering what Bree had told her about the possibility of bursting her lungs, Nancy was careful to exhale gradually, matching her breathing to the decreasing water pressure.

Their swift ascent startled the sniper. His

second shot went wild. Bree guided Nancy directly beneath the boat. Barnacled wood met Nancy's outstretched palms.

Relief washed through Nancy's body. The perfect hiding place! So long as they stayed directly beneath the boat, there was no way the sniper could get at them.

Suddenly the boat's twin propeller began twirling. Its hull lumbered forward. Nancy pushed herself out of harm's way. The cruiser surged past, heading out to sea.

As Nancy surfaced in its wake, she caught a glimpse of the gilt-edged name on the stern. Her blood seemed to freeze all at once. *Sous le Vent.*

It was the boat from the scrap yard—the one that had departed right after the murder attempt.

New questions flooded her mind. Was Henri Chaumette, the boat's owner, the one behind that stunt with the crane? She thought about those boat-shoe prints near the waterfall. Was he also the man behind the spear gun? And if so, why? Who was Henri Chaumette?

Nancy treaded water, watching the boat speed away. There was nothing she could do to pursue it. As she headed back to their boat, a sudden realization made Nancy quicken her strokes. She had to return to the hotel. If the enemy was willing to risk another daylight attack, Nancy had to be on the right track!

An hour later Nancy steered the Renault through the broad gates of Faretaha. Bree sat moodily in the passenger seat. Both girls had exchanged their maillots and scuba gear for tank tops and walking shorts.

Setting the brake, Nancy suggested, "Why don't you wait here? I think I can get more out of Kristin if I face her alone."

Bree gritted her teeth but said nothing. Nancy slammed the car door and bent to look through the window at Bree, a smile playing on her lips.

Bree was too upset to respond in kind though. "Can you blame me for being angry?" She fell silent again.

Nancy exhaled deeply. "I know how you feel, Bree. That's why you're going to sit here until you cool off. Kristin may be innocent, you know."

Still fuming, Bree looked away. "I doubt it!"

"Cool off—please?" Nancy added in a conciliatory tone. "I'll be right back."

Bree nodded curtly, her mouth taut. Nancy wasn't at all sure Bree meant to stay put, but there was nothing she could do about it right then. Shouldering her bag, she strode purposefully up the walk.

She found Kristin standing in the parlor, sipping a late-afternoon drink. The actress was wearing a sleeveless silk top and white silk harem-style trousers. Her lush blond hair curled loosely over shoulders. She glanced suspiciously at Nancy. "What do you want?"

"I'm looking for Bree," Nancy replied, using

the cover story she'd prepared. "I couldn't find her at the hotel, so I thought she might be here."

Kristin smiled sourly. "I'm afraid the spoiled Miss Gordon spends as little time in my company as possible."

Kristin's shoulder dipped awkwardly as she started across the room, and Nancy realized that the actress was limping! Her gaze moved to Kristin's slender ankle, where a pressure bandage was just visible under the trouser cuff.

"How did you hurt your ankle, Ms. Stromm?" she asked, her mind racing. The spear-gun sniper had skidded in the mud while running away, according to those footprints Nancy had found. He or she could easily have twisted an ankle.

Kristin seemed shaken by the question. A nervous smile molded her mouth. "I—I pulled a tendon playing tennis with Bree." Her fingers trembled as she fiddled with her pendant earring. "Surely you remember. You were there."

Right, thought Nancy. *And* I was here at dinner the next night, when there was absolutely nothing wrong with your ankle! She made a mental note to find out whether Kristin owned a pair of boating shoes.

Right now, though, there was another angle to explore. Nancy closed the door behind her and took a step forward. "I don't mean to be rude, but I can't help noticing that you and Bree don't get along very well," she said as tactfully as she could.

"That's not *my* fault!" Kristin's hand brushed the silk cowl of her blouse. "Heaven knows I've tried to be civil to her. She resents me because I'm engaged to her father." A petulant expression marred her lovely face. "I wish she'd get over it! It's not as if I'd cast a net over Brian, you know. We fell in love with each other. Now, tell me, is that a crime?" Her blue eyes flashed fire. "You know what Bree's problem is? She's spoiled rotten. And she's just like her mother— stubborn, mean—"

And that's the real reason you dislike Bree, Nancy realized. Every time you look at her, you see Lucinda.

Keeping that thought to herself, Nancy offered a sympathetic smile. "You didn't like Bree's mother much?" she probed.

"Lucinda Prado was a conceited, conniving witch!" Kristin burst out. "She was jealous of me, you know. She tried to ruin my career!"

At that moment the door banged open, and Bree stormed into the room. "I heard that!" she cried. "Don't listen to her, Nancy. My mother had more talent in her little finger than Krissy'll *ever* have. The only thing Krissy's any good at is stealing other people's husbands!"

Nancy was horrified. Bree was about to blow everything! She held out a placating hand. "Bree—" she began. But Kristin cut her off.

"And just what is that supposed to mean, dear?" she purred. Her voice had a dangerous note.

"You should know!" Bree flung back. "Everybody saw you draping yourself all over my dad the night Mother died. Everybody saw them fighting—over you. And everybody knows where you went later. In fact, if it hadn't been for you, my mother would be alive today!" Glaring at Kristin, Bree turned and left, slamming the door behind her.

Nancy winced. Oh, Bree, she thought. Now you've made yourself a real enemy. And you've ruined my chances of getting any leads here!

"Bree's just being silly, of course," Kristin put in before Nancy could say anything. She waved a careless hand. "I had—I had an appointment to keep that night."

"An appointment at the Café Chat Noir?" Nancy asked in a casual voice. She watched Kristin intently to see how she would react.

Her words had a dramatic effect. Kristin looked as if she'd just been slapped in the face. "Who's been spreading those lies about me?" she screamed. "If Manda—I'll kill that woman!"

"It wasn't Manda," Nancy replied. "I saw you there myself."

Kristin's pale blue eyes widened in alarm. "Who sent you to spy on me?" she shrieked. "Was it Rupert?"

Rupert! Nancy was taken by surprise. Where did the producer fit in to all this? What was his connection to Kristin Stromm?

A door slammed behind them. Turning, Nancy

saw Brian Gordon in the entryway. His face seemed chiseled from stone.

"Darling!" Kristin rushed into his arms. "Don't believe a word she says. It's all lies!"

"Calm down, Kristin." Gently but firmly Brian moved his fiancée to one side. Then he bore down on Nancy. "I hear you've been snooping around, Ms. Drew."

Nancy took a deep breath. She could tell this wasn't going to be easy. "I—"

"I thought I made it clear to you that my wife's death was not open for discussion," Brian interrupted. His eyebrows tightened angrily behind his horn-rimmed glasses. "And yet I hear you've been working behind my back. Manda told me how you questioned her, and I can guess what kind of things you've been asking Kristin." His forefinger stabbed once at Nancy. "What's the story, Ms. Drew? Who are you? A reporter searching for an exclusive? Is that why you befriended my daughter? Or maybe you plan to write a book on the 'inside story' of the *Southwind* disaster?"

Nancy could feel her own temper rising, and she had to struggle to keep it in check. In a level voice, she responded, "Wrong on all counts, Mr. Gordon. I'm—"

"Save it!" Brian thrust his fist at the doorway. "I want you out of this house—now. And if you're still on this island at this time tomorrow, I promise you, you'll be the sorriest girl in the whole South Pacific!"

Chapter

Eleven

"DAD!" BREE'S VOICE rang out.

Peering around Brian, Nancy spied Bree in the doorway. Obviously she had heard Brian shouting and come back to see what was happening.

Brian frowned at his daughter. "This friend of yours has been stirring up a lot of trouble, Bree."

"I asked her to, Dad." Features grim, Bree entered the parlor. "Nancy's a detective. I invited her here."

Brian looked astounded. "What?"

"Someone was sending hate mail to my dorm. They hinted that there was something suspicious about Mother's death," Bree explained. "Whoever they were, they were *right*. Mother was murdered!"

Brian's face paled. "That's not possible."

Nancy grimaced slightly. Bree's tipping off her father—and Kristin—to the real reason for her presence probably would make her job harder. But there was nothing to do.

"I'm afraid Bree's right, Mr. Gordon," Nancy said. "The two of us went looking for Tayo Kapali. Instead we found a package Tayo had hidden for Bree. In it was proof of your wife's murder. Someone cut the *Southwind*'s anchor chain. Tayo found the chain, but he was killed before he could do anything about it."

Brian's gaze traveled from his daughter to Nancy. In his eyes Nancy could see shock and pain warring with something else. Was this the look of a man who had murdered his wife? Nancy just couldn't tell.

After a second Brian regained his composure. "Why come to Kristin?"

"She was at the party that night, that's all, Mr. Gordon." Nancy knew she couldn't push her suspicions too hard at this point. She turned to the Swedish actress. "Ms. Stromm, won't you tell us the truth about where you went after you left your party?"

"No! I can't!" Kristin shook her head stubbornly.

"Why not?" Bree snapped.

"She's not the police." Kristin's desperate gaze avoided Nancy. "I don't have to tell her anything."

Brian hovered protectively beside his fiancée. "Believe me, Ms. Drew, Kristin had nothing to do with Lucinda's death. You're barking up the wrong tree."

Nancy's lips tightened. She was tempted to ask Brian Gordon where *he* had gone that night. But, for Bree's sake, she held her tongue.

Bree was under no such self-restraint. "Dad! What are you doing? *Make* Krissy tell the truth!"

Kristin clutched his arm. "Brian! Don't let these girls badger me like this! Do something!"

"Dad! Don't you care what happened to Mother?" Anguish sounded in Bree's voice.

Nancy read the sheer helplessness in Brian's eyes. Bree's father seemed paralyzed by indecision, his gaze darting everywhere at once.

Frustrated by her father's silence, Bree turned on Kristin. "You killed my mother!"

Brian grabbed his daughter's wrist and pulled her around to face him. In a low voice he said, "Bree, please listen. Kristin didn't kill your mother. You've got to believe me."

Bursting into tears, Bree pulled her wrist loose. "Well, I guess we know whose side *you're* on, don't we?"

She fled outside, weeping uncontrollably. Nancy stood there, torn between going to comfort the girl and questioning her suspects. Then she made up her mind. She could quiz Brian and Kristin anytime. Right now, though, Bree needed a friend.

Heartsick, Nancy left the house. Things certainly looked bleak. Lucinda had been Kristin's chief rival and worst enemy. And now it appeared that their rivalry had extended to Lucinda's husband, as well. Kristin might have killed Bree's mother so she could marry Brian.

Then again, it could just as easily be the other way around. Brian might have killed his wife so he could be with Kristin. Nancy sincerely hoped that wasn't the case. How would poor Bree ever be able to live with it?

Nancy found the girl on the windswept beach. Bree was sitting on a driftwood log, hunched over, sobbing into her upraised hands. Kneeling down, Nancy opened her shoulder bag and withdrew a tissue.

"He knows, Nancy." Eyes shiny with tears, Bree blew her nose. "My father. He knows Kristin killed Mother. He's covering up for her."

"Thank you, Sherlock. This is the wildest leap of illogic I've ever heard," Nancy scolded gently, handing her a fresh tissue.

"Kristin left the house, and—"

"That's all we know," Nancy interrupted quietly. Bree was too emotional right then to see that she had no real proof for what she was saying. "Let's find out where she went before we start accusing her of murder."

Bree dabbed at her eyes. "Innocent people have nothing to hide. Why don't they level with us?"

Nancy had no answer to that one. Squeezing Bree's shoulder, she stood up. "Want me to drive you back to Papeete?"

Bree shook her head, frowning. "I—I just want to be by myself for a while—if you don't mind."

"All right. I'll be back at the car."

Nancy walked slowly across the spacious lawn. A hot breeze ruffled her hair, blowing reddish gold strands into her face. She brushed them away, lost in thought.

Things certainly looked bad for Kristin and Brian. Yet Nancy was reluctant to point a finger just yet. There were still too many loose ends in this case.

Rupert Holmberg, for instance. Three million dollars was an excellent motive, but how was he linked to Kristin? Why did Kristin accuse Nancy of being Rupert's spy after she mentioned the Chat Noir?

Speaking of the café, what about Pierre Panchaud? Why did he lie about not going there? Was it because he didn't want anyone to think he gambled? That didn't seem very likely. But then what was he hiding?

Then there was Manda Withers, who certainly acted like someone with something to hide. Nancy wondered if Manda had known of Kristin's feelings for Brian. Manda might have killed Lucinda, hoping to pin the blame on Kristin.

Finally there were the letters. Who wrote

them? And why hadn't he come right out and said what he had to say?

No, there were still too many unanswered questions. Plenty of digging remained to be done.

Perspiration moistened Nancy's hairline. Her mouth tasted like beach sand. Thinking in the tropic sunshine was thirsty work.

Fortunately, there was a tiny village half a mile down the road, just beyond Faretaha's coconut groves. She remembered seeing an open-air store there.

A few minutes later Nancy stepped under the store's awning. The owner and his wife occupied a dining table, listening to a battered transistor radio. Nancy greeted them in simple French, handed over a few francs, and helped herself to a soda from the ice chest.

Sipping the frosty liquid, Nancy wandered outside and leaned against the rusting steel railing at the edge of the village's busy waterfront.

Fifty feet away lay the main boatyard. Workmen toiled with sandblasters and chisels. Chainsaws sang. Squawking sea gulls patrolled the boatyard.

Nancy's gaze skimmed the racing sloops and workaday cruisers. All at once she spied a familiar-looking superstructure amid the jumble of boats. Her sharp gaze zeroed in. A small cabin cruiser lay tucked away in a narrow canal. And its name was *Sous le Vent!*

Nancy tossed her soda bottle in a nearby trash

bin. No doubt about it. She'd know that cruiser anywhere.

Its owner had chosen a good hideaway, all but invisible from the main highway. From a distance the *Sous le Vent* looked like one of the vessels in the boatyard.

Leaving the railing, Nancy circled the dockside area. She decided to act as if she were out for a casual walk.

Nancy moved quietly. Reaching the end of a lumber pile, she peered around the corner and saw the cruiser sitting in placid water. Opaque curtains shielded its windows. The hull's creaking was the only sound.

Crouched low, Nancy dashed over to a pile of oil barrels. She peeked around the side. The *Sous le Vent* looked deserted.

She listened carefully. A taut rope hummed. Wavelets splashed against the hull.

Nancy approached the canal's edge, then paused as she gauged the distance between dock and boat. A running leap put Nancy on deck. She immediately flattened against the cabin, waiting to see if anyone emerged.

Nothing. No one.

Nancy made her way aft, then halted before the cabin's door. Her heart was pounding as her hand rotated the aluminum doorknob. After a quarter turn it stopped. Locked!

She studied the lock and was in luck. Checking to see if she was being watched, Nancy took out her wallet and removed her plastic library card.

She eased the card into the gap. The plastic slid beneath the latch. She thrust her hand upward. Click! The cabin door swung open.

The vinyl curtains cast an eerie green light. A wave of heat washed over her. The breezeway's glass door was shut. Nancy guessed that the boat had been closed up much of the day.

An open cardboard box occupied the settee. Japanese lettering covered the side. Sifting through the mass of Styrofoam chips, Nancy's fingers made contact with a Teflon-coated object.

She pulled it out and held it up to the light. Tiny wires littered the surface like a golden spiderweb.

Nancy gasped. This must be a system card, the advanced computer device she had overheard the police talking about. What was it doing aboard the *Sous le Vent?*

Outside, a mooring line groaned in protest. Nancy felt the floor shift ever so slightly beneath her feet.

Someone had just boarded the boat!

Stuffing the system card in her purse, Nancy silently made her way aft. She flattened herself against the bulkhead, keeping her gaze on the door.

Soft footsteps sounded. She stared at the door-knob. It began to turn.

Suddenly a cool breeze broke Nancy's concentration. She frowned in confusion. Wasn't the cabin sealed?

Too late, she heard the hushed sound of the breezeway door sliding open.

Behind me!

Nancy's head swiveled, but she was a split second too slow. Something came whistling out of the shadows.

Nancy's consciousness rode a roller coaster of dazzling fireworks. Then it plunged into blackness.

Chapter

Twelve

AT FIRST NANCY was aware of distant sounds. The tinkle of cutlery. The rattle of dishware. The scraping of chairs on a wooden floor.

Then the smells began to register. The oily stink of drying paint. The pungent odor of French cuisine.

Nancy groaned. Her eyes fluttered open.

She was suddenly aware of a thundering headache. She moaned again.

Through bleary eyes, Nancy studied her surroundings. She was slumped in a straight-back chair. Ropes confined her wrists. Gray fuse boxes hung from one wall. Thick metallic cables crossed the room from a sturdy engine to an opening on the opposite wall. Freshly painted stage scenery occupied the far wall.

Nancy tried to reconcile the room's backstage appearance with the restaurant noises beyond. Then she spied a stairwell leading down to a gambling casino.

Of course! Nancy thought. The Chat Noir has a stage. I must be in one of the back rooms.

Nancy grimaced at the intensity of her headache. Sitting up, she felt hemp tighten and bite into her ankles and chest.

Just then, footsteps sounded on the stairwell. Two men marched into the room, toting boxes with Japanese calligraphy. Nancy's eyes flickered in recognition. Her two friends from the Chat Noir—Thin Face and Black Beret.

Ripping open a box, Thin Face remarked, "This is the last of them, eh?"

"Yes. There'll be another shipment next month." Black Beret glanced at his watch. "We'd better hurry though. That ship leaves for Valparaiso with the tide change." An evil smile twisted his mouth as he glanced at Nancy. "Well, well, look who's back with us again."

"Little Miss Deuxième Bureau." Thin Face cruelly tweaked Nancy's chin. She recoiled from his touch. "I still say we should have dumped her in the canal."

Black Beret scooped a handful of system cards out of his box. "She'll be feeding the fish soon enough. You heard what the boss said. She dies —but not around the boat."

103

Nancy rotated her wrists, trying to work some slack into her bonds. "Would your boss's name, by any chance, be Henri Chaumette?"

Black Beret blinked in astonishment.

Thin Face laughed out loud. "Hey, Chaumette!" he cackled. "She knows your *brother.*"

"Shut up, Brumaire! You talk too much." The big man loomed over Nancy. "You think you're clever, don't you? Sneaking aboard our boat in search of evidence. How'd you find out about the *Sous le Vent,* eh?"

"I kept seeing it around." Nancy relaxed in her chair. It was no use—the knots were too tight. "Was that you with the spear gun? Or was it Henri?"

Brumaire's thin face snarled in disgust. "That fool! I told you we should've let the boat stay where it was!"

"Shut up, idiot! When are you going to learn? Don't chat around cops." Chaumette tossed him a computer part. "Here, make yourself useful. I'll see that this one won't cause any more trouble." He picked up a roll of thick, silver gaffer's tape and cut a strip. He said nothing but smiled as he placed it over Nancy's mouth.

Nancy now watched helplessly as the two men brought in a crate of ripe breadfruit. With painstaking care, they pushed a system card through each fruit's pulpy skin.

I must have stumbled onto the smugglers Captain Mutoi was looking for, Nancy realized. She tilted her head back. It was so hard to think with a headache.

Here was another piece of the puzzle. But it made no sense. The *Sous le Vent* was the killer's boat. Twice it had been used in murder attempts against her and Bree. Yet the smugglers acted as if it were theirs.

The Café Chat Noir was the key, she knew. That's where she had first encountered the smugglers. Pierre Panchaud was a regular customer. Kristin Stromm did her gambling there. And, judging from Kristin's outburst, Rupert Holmberg had something to do with the café as well.

But Nancy just couldn't see a link between Lucinda Prado's murder and the computer smugglers.

"There!" Brumaire hoisted a breadfruit crate onto his shoulder. "Let's get this stuff down to the docks."

"Right!" Chaumette sneered at Nancy. "Then we can take care of this little snooper."

The two trudged down the stairwell. The door slammed, cutting off Nancy's view of the casino.

I've got to free myself, she thought desperately. Chaumette and Brumaire won't be gone for long!

An electric guitar twanged. Heavy footsteps trod the stage beyond the wall. Nancy heard a baritone voice. "The last show of the night, boys. Let's make it good."

Behind her the engine clattered to life. The cables began to vibrate. Nancy had an idea!

105

The band onstage was about to raise the curtains. When they did so, the cables would start to move. Nancy noticed that the cables' metallic texture was as rough as sandpaper.

Nancy's fingers curled around the edge of her chair. Her sneaker soles pressed the floor. The tape on her mouth muffled the grunts of her effort as she jockeyed her chair back, one inch at a time, closer to the cable.

The engine picked up speed.

Ropes bit into her ankles. Ignoring the pain, Nancy shoved the chair back again and again. Gears engaged. The cables began to move. The humming reached a crescendo. Gasping, Nancy threw herself backward. The chair tottered on its hind legs, then came to rest against the cable.

A buzzsaw sound reached Nancy's ears. The ropes around her chest went slack. Leaning forward, she lifted her bound wrists. The thrumming cable ate into the ropes. Hemp began to fray.

Just then the cable quivered to a halt. Nancy exhaled deeply. The curtain must have reached the top.

Gathering all her strength, Nancy strained against her frayed bonds. One by one the weakened strands parted.

After untying her ankles and pulling the tape painfully from her mouth, Nancy hobbled over to the stairwell. Painful pins and needles prickled her legs.

As soon as her circulation was back, Nancy

picked her way down the stairs. She tried the door, the only entrance to that backstage room. Relief washed through her. The smugglers hadn't bothered to lock it.

Nancy swiftly made her way through the casino. White sheets covered the dice tables and roulette wheel. Rock music serenaded her all the way to the door.

Opening it a crack, Nancy peered into the main dining area. A busboy cleared an abandoned table. Otherwise, the place seemed empty.

Dropping to her hands and knees, Nancy crawled into the dining room. Crouching, she moved gradually toward the front door from table to table, hiding whenever the busboy walked by.

All at once Nancy heard masculine laughter. She peered over the top of the neighboring table.

Rupert Holmberg and the maître d' stood together in the foyer. Chuckling to himself, Rupert counted out several large-denomination francs and placed them in the maître d's outstretched hand.

All smiles, the maître d' crooned, "It's always a pleasure doing business with you, Monsieur Holmberg."

"You've always been a very great help to me, Marcel," the producer replied. "See what else you can dig up, eh?"

Nancy studied them intently. Could Rupert be the mysterious boss the smugglers had mentioned?

Putting on his Panama hat, Rupert sauntered out of the café. Marcel carefully counted his loot, then tucked the wad into his back pocket.

Minutes later Chaumette and Brumaire appeared. The maître d' flashed them an impatient look. "It's about time you two got back."

"Don't be nervous, Marcel." Chaumette showed him a smirk. "We weren't going to leave the girl with you."

Sweating apprehensively, Marcel mopped his brow with a handkerchief. "You shouldn't have brought her here at all."

"Don't worry!" Brumaire slapped the maître d's back heartily. "She's coming with us to South America. Well—halfway, at least." He snickered. "Sharks have to eat too."

Nancy held her breath as the smugglers drifted toward her table, laughing at their private joke. She ducked behind the white tablecloth.

Suddenly the kitchen doors swung open behind her. The busboy hurried in, exclaiming, "Dishes are all done, Marcel. Can I go?" Halting, he stared in bewilderment at Nancy. "Hey! What are you doing?"

Blood freezing, Nancy peeped over the tabletop. The two smugglers were staring right at her!

"She got loose!" Brumaire whipped out a switchblade. "Get her!"

Chapter

Thirteen

NANCY BOLTED INTO ACTION. Zipping around the neighboring table, she dashed into the casino. Angry footfalls echoed behind her. She slammed the door shut.

Her gaze found the deadbolt. She thrust it home just as a heavy weight crashed into the door, rocking it on its hinges. There were two more crashes but the stout door held.

Nancy stepped away. The locked door had bought her a few minutes' reprieve, but that was all. They'd soon find something to break it down with.

Her spirits sank. She was trapped. The only other door led to the stairs up to the backstage room where she'd been tied up.

Refusing to give up, Nancy pulled the sheets from the gaming tables. There had to be something she could use as a weapon. Ivory dice mocked her.

Nothing!

The door vibrated under the impact of each savage assault. Nancy clenched her fists, thinking furiously.

Her gaze kept returning to that backstage room. If she could only trick them into going up there, she might be able to get the upper hand.

Nancy's hand closed around a pair of dice. She ducked under the roulette table.

Crash! The casino door splintered open.

"Search the room!" Chaumette bellowed. "She's got to be hiding here somewhere."

Nancy knew her cue. Turning, she flung the dice through the open door. Ivory cubes clattered noisily on the stairs.

"She's in there!" Brumaire cried.

Nancy watched as the two smugglers stormed the stairway. Then, scrambling to her feet, she rushed across the room, slammed the stairway door, and dropped the sidebar, locking it.

Realizing they had been tricked, the smugglers bellowed in rage. Angry fists hammered the door.

Hasty footsteps caught Nancy's attention. Looking to the left, she spied the maître d' trying to sneak out.

Coming up behind him, Nancy tapped him on the shoulder. "Not so fast, Marcel! I know a police captain who'd like to talk to you."

Marcel flinched at her touch, his pudgy face turning pale. Nancy could see that he vividly remembered her karate demonstration.

"Don't hit me!" he pleaded.

"Behave yourself and I won't," Nancy replied, trying hard not to grin. "Now let's go make a phone call."

Ten minutes later the late-night street outside the café was full of police cars. Nancy watched in satisfaction as the khaki-clad officers marched the smugglers out to a waiting van.

Just then, a familiar male voice sounded behind her. "I seem to have underestimated you, Mademoiselle Drew. I've been looking for you." Captain Mutoi's expression was aloof but friendly. "Bree Gordon called me late this afternoon. When you didn't return to Faretaha, she became quite concerned. The young lady and I had an interesting conversation." He glanced at the van. "How did you catch those two?"

"Actually, they caught me aboard their boat, the *Sous le Vent,*" Nancy explained. "The café is their home base. They had a batch of Japanese computer parts in there earlier. Now they've loaded them onto a ship bound for South America." Nancy felt a small rush of pride as the officer gave her a look that said he was impressed.

Captain Mutoi ordered two men to the waterfront to search the ship. Then he walked Nancy out of the café.

"After I talked to Mademoiselle Gordon, I had the lab take a look at that anchor chain. They tell me it was cut," he said matter-of-factly. "I hope you'll accept my apology—for doubting you, that is." A wry smile unfolded on his handsome face.

"That's quite all right. I understand."

Captain Mutoi's smile turned thoughtful. "Now that you've helped me with my big case, perhaps I can return the favor. How are you making out on the Prado murder?"

Nancy quickly brought him up-to-date. When she was finished, he commented, "Who did you say the *Sous le Vent* belonged to?"

"Henri Chaumette, the smuggler's brother."

"Brumaire was making a joke," Captain Mutoi replied. "I know those two. Chaumette has no brother. The name Henri must be an alias."

A frown creased Nancy's brow. An alias? That put a different light on things.

The connections were still there. The killer owned the *Sous le Vent* under an assumed name. The two smugglers used the boat, as well. All three were tied to the Chat Noir.

And so were Kristin, Pierre, and Rupert. Fatigue washed over Nancy like a tidal wave. She was too tired to puzzle it out now. Stifling a yawn with her palm, she murmured, "I'm afraid I'm ready to drop."

Captain Mutoi gestured at a waiting police cruiser. "I'll drive you back to the Taravao. In the morning we'll see if we can't get to the bottom of this mystery."

* * *

The following day Nancy, Bree, and Captain Mutoi drove out to Faretaha. On the way Bree explained that her father had chosen to stay there overnight rather than return to Papeete.

Nancy said nothing. She could see how this case was affecting Bree. The girl's eyes were red rimmed, and her face was a mask of sheer misery. Suspicion had opened an ugly breach between father and daughter.

On arrival they walked up the front lane together. Then Captain Mutoi's fist sounded a brisk tattoo on the oak door.

Manda Withers answered the door. She had obviously accompanied her employer. Surprise flickered in her brown eyes. Brian Gordon appeared behind her, looking older than his years. Behind him, Kristin sat on the sofa, watching apprehensively.

Brian cast Nancy a somber glance. "So you've brought the police. I figured you would."

Captain Mutoi held out his right hand. "I shall have to ask you and Mademoiselle Stromm to surrender your passports, monsieur."

Brian reached into his inside pocket. Sighing, he handed the document over. "For what it's worth, I didn't kill my wife."

Kristin swallowed hard. "Brian, please don't tell them. Think—think of the humiliation."

"Sorry, Krissy." Drawing his shoulders back, he gave Bree a long look. "But if my daughter's going to hate me, she might as well hate me for the right reason."

113

Nancy realized that Bree might be hurt by the answer. Still, the question had to be asked.

"Mr. Gordon, where were you the night your wife was killed?"

He took a long moment to answer. "I was with Kristin."

Bree let out an anguished gasp.

"It's not what you think." Brian's shoulders seemed to sink under a heavy weight.

Lifting his head, Brian sighed once more. "Kristin came up to me at the party. She asked me to help her. Lucinda saw the two of us talking and lost her temper. I told Lucinda she was being rude. Next thing you know, we're going at it hammer and tongs again. Then she stormed out." He rubbed the back of his neck gingerly. "The party broke up after that. I had a cigarette in the garden. Then I ran across Kristin. She was crying. I sat her down on a bench—asked her what was wrong."

Nancy glanced at the actress. Tears were welling up in Kristin's eyes.

"Krissy has always liked to gamble," Brian added. "Five years ago, however, she got in way over her head. She thought she was going to lose Faretaha. Then Rupert Holmberg entered the picture."

Rupert! Excitement prickled along Nancy's neck. "Go on."

"Rupert found out about Krissy's debts," Brian explained. "He paid them himself. Then he offered her a special business arrangement. He would cancel her debts if she signed an exclusive, three-year contract with him."

"What were the terms of the contract?" asked Nancy.

"He wanted Krissy to do five movies for him, working at union scale—the lowest wage possible," he explained. "Krissy's career was just starting to take off back then. *Horizon of Desire* had just made a bundle. Rupert would have owned Krissy outright."

Nancy made a guess. "So you two went to see Rupert."

"I couldn't just stand there and see Krissy's career destroyed," Brian said, lifting his chin in pride. "So I confronted Rupert, tried to pressure him."

Captain Mutoi scribbled in his notebook. "And then what happened?"

"Rupert and I argued for a couple of hours. I threatened to blow the whistle on him. He said he'd turn Krissy's debts over to people who wouldn't be as considerate as he was. We finally hammered out a deal. I promised to direct one of his future films, and Lucinda would star in it. We signed a memorandum of agreement to that effect."

Nancy nodded in understanding. Now she could see why Brian had been so reluctant to discuss his wife's death.

"You must believe me." Brian stared directly at his daughter. "I loved your mother very much. Kristin was only an acquaintance then. I was a long time getting over Lucinda's death. I didn't know I was going to fall in love with Kristin. It just happened."

Eyes downcast, Bree turned her face away.

"One thing puzzles me," Nancy observed. "If Rupert is such a sleaze, why are you still friends with him?"

Brian bristled at that. "I'm not *friends* with him, Nancy. I put up with him, that's all. Technically speaking, I still owe him a movie."

Captain Mutoi cleared his throat. "Monsieur, would you happen to have a copy of this memorandum of agreement?"

"It's with my other papers." Brian led them all to the library. Kristin hobbled along behind them. "I had Manda bring them out here this morning. Figured I'd get a little work done while I was here."

But as they entered the library, a stunning sight met their collective gaze.

Manda was standing beside the fireplace, a manila folder in her left hand. Her right gripped a silver cigarette lighter. Its wick burst into flame.

"Manda!" shouted Brian, too late.

Manda's quaking hand shoved the lighter against the folder. All at once a sheet of fire rippled up its side!

Chapter

Fourteen

Rushing forward, Nancy knocked the blazing folder out of Manda's grasp. It fluttered to the carpet. Nancy stamped out the flames.

Stooping, she flipped open the charred folder. The letter was brown around the edges but still readable. The Holmberg Cinema Productions logo ran across the top of the page.

Nancy's gaze skimmed the typescript.

This document certifies and attests that Brian Gordon shall direct, and Lucinda Prado shall star in, a film project for Holmberg Cinema Productions within the next seven years. In return for the services listed heretofore, Rupert Holmberg will destroy all instruments of debt in his possession relating to Kristin Stromm. The undersigned readily and without reservation agree to consent to the provisions listed above.

Brian and Rupert's signatures punctuated the text. Nancy checked the date. Brian hadn't lied. This memorandum had been drawn up the night of the *Southwind*'s fatal collision.

Captain Mutoi studied it over Nancy's shoulder, then gave Brian an ironic smile. "You are most fortunate, monsieur. It's still clearly readable."

"You idiot!" Brian grabbed his secretary's shoulders. "What are you trying to do?"

Manda burst into tears. "I—I thought I could help you by destroying the evidence."

"That evidence is the only thing that can clear me!" Deeply shaken, Brian pointed at the door. "Out, Manda! You're fired!"

"It *may* clear you, Monsieur Gordon—*if* this man Holmberg backs up your story." The captain ushered Bree and her father outside. "Why don't you all wait in the hall? Mademoiselle Drew and I will speak to this woman alone."

Nancy held the door for Kristin. "If you don't mind another question—how did you sprain your ankle?" she asked quietly.

Embarrassment painted Kristin's face a deep crimson. "I twisted it running away from the café the other night. I—I didn't want to be arrested in the police raid."

118

Why hadn't she guessed? Nancy smiled to herself as she closed the door and rejoined the captain.

Manda sat on the armrest of a couch, looking like a little girl on her way to the principal's office. Grim-faced Captain Mutoi made a good stand-in for the principal.

"How could he do it?" Manda sobbed. "How could he fire me that way?"

"Mademoiselle, believe me, that is the *least* of your problems," Captain Mutoi said sternly. "You were caught in the act of destroying evidence in a murder case. For that alone you could spend the next year in our prison."

Wailing in misery, Manda buried her face in her hands.

Nancy cast a sympathetic look at the weeping woman. "What about extenuating circumstances, Captain?"

Captain Mutoi offered her a quizzical look. "You know the reason for her behavior?"

Nancy nodded slowly. "Manda's in love with Bree's father. She has been for years. That's why she tried to burn Rupert's memo. And that's why she sent those unsigned letters to Bree."

Guilt turned the secretary's face pale. "H-How did you know *that?*"

"It wasn't too hard to figure out, Ms. Withers," Nancy replied. "Especially knowing how you feel about Brian. Those letters all had Tahiti postmarks. You knew Bree would recognize your handwriting, so you used a ruler to disguise it."

"I seem to have missed something," Captain Mutoi remarked dryly.

After explaining about the letters, Nancy added, "Ms. Withers thought Kristin was all wrong for Brian. So she mailed those letters to Bree, hinting at some nasty secret about her mother's death. She figured that if she could turn Bree against Kristin, Bree would persuade her father to call off the wedding."

"I-I'm sorry." Manda sobbed. "I c-couldn't stand it, seeing Brian with Kristin—"

"And people in love do crazy things sometimes," Nancy concluded softly, kneeling before the couch. She smiled in sympathy. "I think you'd better tell us everything."

Captain Mutoi stepped closer. "Unrequited love can be a powerful motive for murder." He looked down at Manda. "Did you kill Lucinda Prado?"

All color fled Manda's face. "No! I swear it!"

"Ms. Withers," Nancy said gently. "You were missing from Kristin's estate that night." At Manda's shocked gaze, she explained, "Bree woke up in the middle of the night. She went looking for you, but the house was deserted."

Wiping away tears, Manda murmured, "You're right. After the others left, I went looking for Brian. I saw him in the garden—with *Kristin!*" Her fists clenched angrily. "I was so furious. If he wanted comforting, why didn't he come to *me?*

"I drove back to Papeete, intending to make

him pay. I planned to row out to the *Southwind* and tell Lucinda." She looked thoroughly chastened.

"I walked up and down the beach, looking for a dinghy. There weren't any. My nerve began to fail me. What would happen if I told? Lucinda had such a temper, you see. I was afraid she might hurt him physically! I—I only wanted to make life a little bit miserable for Brian. I didn't want him hurt! So I changed my mind and left." Her voice began to break. "That's why I tried to burn those files. I couldn't bear the thought of Brian being hurt. I *love* him."

Nancy thought back to her interviews with the *Southwind* witnesses. So Manda was the mystery woman Alistair Pendleton had seen that night.

Nancy shook her head. She had thought she was on the brink of unraveling the mystery, but this new revelation raised more questions than it answered. According to Manda and Pendleton, there were no small boats left ashore after Lucinda departed for her yacht. If that were true, then how did the killer get out to the *Southwind?*

"Manda, what time did you get to the beach?" asked Nancy.

"Two o'clock, I think."

Nancy's brows knit thoughtfully. "You're certain that you didn't see any dinghies ashore?"

"None. The beach was deserted." Pursing her lips painfully, Manda aimed a timid glance at the captain. "Will I have to go to prison?"

"That depends." Captain Mutoi squared his shoulders. "We shall see what the judge says, eh?"

Nancy and the captain left Manda in the library alone. After saying goodbye to the Gordons and Kristin, they headed back to the car.

"I think this eliminates Manda as a suspect," Nancy said as they walked along. "Mr. Pendleton saw her leave the beach *before* the *Southwind* was cast adrift."

"Which leaves us with Gordon, Holmberg, and the Stromm woman," Captain Mutoi put in, nodding.

"Not to mention Pierre Panchaud," Nancy said, smiling wearily. "Don't forget. He was on board the *Southwind* all along."

"Ah! But Panchaud has no motive. And he was belowdecks the entire time, remember? He had to be on deck to cut the anchor chain."

Nancy grimaced. Captain Mutoi was right. Pierre had a tight alibi.

"I think, Nancy, we should pay a little visit to Monsieur Holmberg."

Once they reached the car, Captain Mutoi radioed the gendarmerie, requesting the location of Rupert's boat. Four minutes later the dispatcher's voice crackled through the receiver. At last report Rupert's boat, the *Sea Nymph*, was moored in Arue.

To Nancy's surprise, Arue turned out to be the very same village where she had seen the *Sous le Vent.* After parking along the waterfront, Nancy and the captain checked the canal. The smugglers' boat was gone!

Next, Nancy and Captain Mutoi sought out the dockmaster. The young Tahitian pointed out Rupert's boat to them.

A white forty-foot trisail motor schooner with blue trim, the *Sea Nymph* was moored at the main pier. Sunshine gleamed on the boat's brightwork. Her first sight of the elegant vessel surprised Nancy. The *Sea Nymph* didn't seem to fit Rupert's personality at all. And then she remembered that it was an identical copy of the *Southwind,* a craft Rupert had very much admired.

They found Rupert in flashy sunglasses and swim trunks, enjoying a drink as he sprawled on a chaise lounge. Unused scuba gear rested beside the vessel's cabin.

"Look who's here—Nancy Drew." Rupert took a quick sip of his drink, then flashed a welcoming grin. "Who's your friend?"

"Captain Mutoi. He's with the police." Nancy gestured at her companion. "Do you have a minute to talk?"

"Sure." Rupert removed his sunglasses and smiled at his visitors, but Nancy sensed there was nothing friendly in the expression. "I hope this isn't going to take too long. I feel like a swim."

Nancy cast a look at the inviting blue-green water, then turned back to the producer. "I guess Tahiti's been pretty good to you, Mr. Holmberg."

He leaned back, his smile wider than ever. "Truer words were never spoken, Nancy. Hot sun. Sparkling sea. Friendly people." A contented sigh passed his lips. "Heaven!" Opening his eyes again, he glanced at Captain Mutoi. "I'm getting an idea. I think I'll make a Foreign Legion movie. Yeah! What do you say, Nancy? You and your cop friend want to be extras in a remake of *Under Two Flags?*"

Nancy shook her head. "No thanks. I'd rather talk about *your* friend—the maître d' at the Café Chat Noir."

Rupert's smile vanished. His heavy body sat up slowly.

"Me? In the Chat Noir?" Rupert let his hand drift over the side of the lounge chair. "Now, where did you ever get a dumb idea like that?"

"I guess it comes from being at the café myself last night and seeing you pay off Marcel," Nancy replied evenly.

Rupert turned the pale gray of a clamshell.

Nancy confronted him. "Mr. Holmberg, why did you pay him off?"

The producer's hand closed around a spear gun. With a snarl, he swiveled toward them. In an eyeblink the spearhead's razor-sharp tip was pointing at Nancy's throat.

Chapter

Fifteen

BACK OFF!" Rupert barked, jabbing with the spear gun.

Nancy obeyed at once, her breath caught in her throat. Her shoulder blades brushed an upright object. Reaching behind her, she ran her fingertips along its fiberglass length. A fishing pole!

"Looks as if I've worn out my welcome in Tahiti." Rupert's shifty gaze flitted from Nancy to Captain Mutoi. "No matter. Once you two are tied up, I can be on my way."

Suddenly Captain Mutoi lunged at him. Rupert pointed the spear gun at the officer. "Stay back!"

Nancy saw her chance. Grabbing the fishing pole by its heavy end, she caught Rupert sharply on the wrist with the metal reel. Rupert howled. The spear gun clattered to the deck.

Captain Mutoi pinned the yelping producer to the deck. Then, after slipping a pair of handcuffs off his belt, he locked Rupert's wrists behind his back.

"What are you doing?" Rupert hollered. "Hey, I'm a big man in Hollywood!"

"You may have worn out your welcome in Tahiti." Captain Mutoi hauled the producer upright. "But we'd just love to have you at our jungle prison camp in the Tuamotus."

"P-prison?" Sweat trickled down Rupert's face. "Come on, you guys, where's your sense of humor? It was a joke. Honest!" He gazed imploringly at Nancy. "I only wanted to shake you up a little. It was a gag! Ha-ha—ha-ha-ha— See, I'm laughing."

"I'm sure you'll have all the guards in stitches." Captain Mutoi sat him back on the lounge chair. "The young lady asked you a question a moment ago, monsieur."

Listless, Rupert mumbled, "I forget."

"Why did you pay off Marcel?" Nancy prodded.

"I was buying information." Rupert caught their puzzled expressions and explained. "I knew there was a little action going on at the Chat Noir. I figured to spread some money around— find out things."

"What kind of things?"

"Actors are always getting into scrapes," Rupert explained. "It pays to know what kind of trouble they've had. I like to have that kind of insurance when I negotiate contracts with film people."

"Insurance? It sounds more like blackmail to me," Nancy observed. "Why did you put the squeeze on Kristin?"

"I was stuck with a couple of bomb-o movies five years ago," Rupert said, avoiding their stern gaze. "The banks were after my— Ah, you get the idea. Krissy'd just hit it big in *Horizon of Desire.* When I heard about her gambling debts, I made her an offer." Exasperation made him look like a naughty little boy. "Then that do-gooder Gordon stuck his nose in. I hated to lose Krissy, but he made me a good counteroffer. A movie with him directing and Lucinda in the lead was sure to make money."

"But Lucinda planned to retire. She was through with films," Nancy added. "That put you in a real bind, didn't it?"

Rupert realized the significance of Nancy's words. Looking at her askance, he replied, "What are you trying to say?"

"You had a motive, monsieur," put in Captain Mutoi gravely. "A three-million-dollar profit."

"Give me a break!" Rupert wailed, squirming uncomfortably in his seat. "I took a loss on that deal like you wouldn't believe. Three million? That was *peanuts* compared to the dough I would've made if Lucinda had lived. That woman was box-office dynamite!"

"Brian mentioned a memorandum of agreement," Nancy added. "Could we have a look at your copy?"

Huffing and puffing, Rupert rose awkwardly to his feet. "It's below with the rest of my files."

Captain Mutoi kept a firm grip on his shoulder as Rupert led them to the right-hand side of the boat. They descended the teakwood ladder single file, Nancy in the lead.

Minutes later in the master stateroom, Rupert jutted his chin at the file cabinet. Nancy spent several minutes rummaging through the manila folders. Finally one marked Gordon caught her eye.

She flipped it open and looked down at an identical copy of Brian's memorandum.

Nancy turned to the producer. "So Brian and Kristin were with you most of the night."

"Yeah. That's right. They showed up at my beach house about two o'clock or so."

"Where is your beach house?" asked Nancy.

"The other side of the island. Fifteen, twenty miles past Papeete." Rupert shot them a hopeful look. "I helped you out, right? So you're going to let me go, right?"

"Wrong!" Captain Mutoi steered the handcuffed man up the companionway. "You're under arrest, Monsieur Holmberg. That means you're coming with me."

"What!" Rupert balked every step of the way. "Hey, do you know who you're talking to?"

"I'm talking to a man who just confessed to blackmail. Step lively there." Captain Mutoi glanced at Nancy. "Would you care for a lift back to Papeete, mademoiselle?"

Nancy shook her head. Her work here was done. "Thanks, but no. I'll walk back to Faretaha. I want to see how Bree's doing."

"Suit yourself." The captain seized the prisoner's upper arm. *"Au revoir."*

Standing before the galley, Nancy listened to Rupert's desperate pleading. She had to smile in spite of herself.

"C-Captain, you don't really want to take me to jail. Listen, a good-looking guy like you has a great future in the movies. I'm not kidding! You want to be a star? I can make you a star. Come on, talk to me!"

The decisive slam of a car door interrupted the producer's sales pitch. Nancy shook her head, perplexity overcoming the humor of the final scene.

Exhaling wearily, she leaned against the bulkhead. What a case. It was proving to be one of her most difficult. Every single one of the suspects had an alibi.

Brian and Kristin were with Rupert at his beach house, miles away from the *Southwind.* Manda, the mystery woman on the beach, had been seen leaving before the murder. Pierre was on board the *Southwind,* but he had never gone topside.

In fact, Nancy remembered, Pierre Panchaud was in the galley when the *Southwind* was rammed.

Nancy peered through the *Sea Nymph*'s galley hatch. The shining countertops, polished table, and swivel seats seemed to jeer at her. It was as if the galley itself were trying to tell her something.

Frowning impatiently, Nancy drummed the bulkhead with her fingertips. This was crazy! One of the suspects had to be guilty. She had seen the hacksawed anchor chain with her own eyes.

If only it were possible to reconstruct the scene of the crime, Nancy mused. But, of course, the idea was ridiculous. The *Southwind*'s wreckage lay strewn all over the ocean floor.

All at once, Nancy snapped her fingers. What was she thinking of? Of *course* it was possible! Rupert's *Sea Nymph* was an identical copy of the doomed *Southwind*.

As Nancy faced the galley hatchway, Pierre's story ran through her mind.

"I could hear the buoy's bell ringing outside. I looked through one of the portholes and saw the buoy's green light and the big Moorea ferry passing astern . . ."

Suddenly Nancy's eyes went wide. There were no portholes at all in the galley! The hatch would have been closed in a major storm like that. Pierre *couldn't* have seen anything!

A grim smile touched her lips. "Nice try, Pierre!"

Four minutes later Nancy was rushing into

Arue's village store. She went straight to the pay phone, popped in a few coins, and began dialing.

The phone at the other end rang three times. Kristin's voice came on the line. "Hello?"

"Kristin, this is Nancy Drew. Would you please put Bree on? This is very important."

"Oh, she just left. She should be there any minute."

A bolt of fear lanced Nancy's heart. "Bree's coming to see me?"

"Yes. Bree walked out of here five minutes ago. She left with that fellow—I forget his name—the one who used to work on their boat. He told me you sent him to fetch Bree."

"What? I did no such thing!" Nancy replied. "Please do exactly as I say, Kristin. The second I hang up, call the police. Tell them Bree's with Pierre Panchaud. He's the killer!"

Nancy hung up. Heart pounding with apprehension, she rushed into the street. She should have known what Pierre was up to the moment she and Captain Mutoi had found the *Sous le Vent* gone.

I was a little slow on the uptake on this one, Nancy thought. Pierre told me the clue himself, but I didn't realize the significance of it. When he joined the *Southwind*'s crew five years ago, Pierre was in Japan. He was setting up his smuggling ring. The *Sous le Vent* is his boat. He registered it under the alias "Henri Chaumette."

Pierre must have heard about his partners' arrest and put the boat to sea. It was only twelve miles to Moorea, the nearest island. He could have anchored there in safety.

Nancy forced herself to remain calm. If Pierre and Bree had left the estate on foot, then the *Sous le Vent* had to be around here somewhere. Pierre was too smart to stray too far from his only means of escape.

Crossing the street, Nancy jogged along the rusting seaside railing, searching the boatyard for the *Sous le Vent*. Finally, her keen gaze spied a small wharf, half-hidden behind a grove of palm trees. Pierre's boat lay at anchor there, hull creaking as it strained against the mooring lines.

Nancy sneaked aboard, intent on disabling the engine. Then she could call the police. Once again she slipped the cabin latch. There was no response from within. Taking a deep breath, she made her way below.

No sooner had Nancy closed the hatch than she heard muffled voices. The boat shifted in the water as people climbed aboard. Nancy flattened herself against the cabin bulkhead, listening.

"I'm glad you decided to help us, Pierre."

"Ah, you can thank Nancy Drew for that, Bree. After she told me about Tayo's murder, I knew I had to come forward."

Nancy eased the door open a crack. Bree was on the starboard side, looking out to sea. Pierre stood several steps behind her. He opened a box of fishing tackle, studying its interior pensively. Then, as if changing his mind, he set it down on a fisherman's chair and went to free the mooring lines.

Nancy fretted silently. At first she had planned to sabotage Pierre's engine. But she didn't dare leave Bree now!

"I hope Nancy gets here soon," Bree said, letting the breeze ruffle her long black hair.

Pierre stood erect. He held a length of nylon rope in his hands. He snapped it once, testing its strength. Then he slowly wound it round his hands.

"So do I, mademoiselle. So do I."

Nancy's blue eyes flickered in alarm.

Pierre quietly came up right behind Bree. Then he lifted the strangle cord with deadly, ominous precision.

Chapter

Sixteen

Nancy burst out of hiding. "Don't try it, Pierre!"

Astounded, Pierre stepped back. Nancy took advantage of his momentary confusion, pulling an equally startled Bree away from him.

Bree stumbled against her. "Nancy, what are you—?"

"He killed your mother." Nancy pointed at the rope in his hands. "He was just about to strangle you."

Pierre dropped the rope. "You're crazy!"

Nancy aimed her forefinger at him. "Everybody had an alibi. Yours is the best one of all. In fact, it's too good, Pierre."

Pierre's hand drifted toward a box of fishing

tackle. He must have a weapon in there! Nancy realized. She darted forward, then stopped short as Pierre's hand emerged, holding a small snub-nosed automatic pistol. "Too late," he said with a sneer.

Nancy took a deep breath to calm herself. Her only hope now was to try to deflect his attention by talking, stalling him until she could think of a way to get at the weapon.

Careful to make no suspicious movements, she slowly lowered her hands to her sides. "Let's go over your story. You said you saw the green light on the bell buoy and the ferry passing astern. The *Southwind* witnesses told me the same thing. Your stories all meshed. But that's impossible!"

Pierre's trigger finger twitched, and Nancy fought to keep all signs of alarm from her face.

"There's one thing wrong with your story, Pierre," Nancy added quickly. "You can't see any of that from inside the *Southwind*. There are no portholes in the galley. The reason you saw all that is because you were on deck with Lucinda Prado. And you were on deck because you killed her!"

"Why on earth would he want to kill my mother?" asked Bree.

"Pierre was a smuggler," Nancy explained, glancing at Bree. "That's why he signed aboard the *Southwind* in Japan five years ago. He was looking for a way to ship stolen computer parts into Papeete. He knew Lucinda Prado was a big star. The customs people were unlikely to search her yacht that thoroughly. So he stashed his goods aboard and returned to Tahiti with you people."

Pierre glanced murderously at Nancy, but she plunged ahead—anything to keep him occupied. "The night of the storm, Pierre had the whole boat to himself," Nancy went on. "That's when he took those computer parts out of hiding. He probably planned to move them ashore in the morning. But then your mother returned unexpectedly, Bree. She caught Pierre with the goods. She went topside, intending to take the dinghy back to shore and report him to the police. Pierre followed her on deck, came up behind her, and killed her!"

A ghastly expression crossed Pierre's face. Nancy could see that the murder had happened just as she had guessed.

She took advantage of his astonishment to race on. "Pierre had to move fast. He had no way of knowing whether or not your father was right behind," Nancy added. "Pierre realized that the anchor winch would make too much noise. So he took a hacksaw and cut the anchor chain. The *Southwind* went out with the tide. Pierre steered her right into the path of that freighter. Then he took a life preserver and went over the side."

Pierre's eyes were desperate. "I didn't mean to—"

"Tell us another one," Nancy urged, seeing that her account of the events had made him forget the deadly weapon he held. "Just like you didn't mean to put that snake in Bree's bed, right? Or drop that load of scrap on me." Looking down, she noticed that Pierre was wearing boat shoes. "You left some nice clear footprints there and at Vaipahi, when you took that shot at us."

Pierre shuffled, as if trying to escape Nancy's accusatory stare.

"And let's not forget Tayo," Nancy pressed. "You found out he was diving at the *Southwind*'s old anchorage. You're a scuba diver. You checked yourself and found the anchor gone. So the next time Tayo went diving, you cruised by in the *Sous le Vent* and shot him with your spear gun. The sharks did the rest."

"You're a smart little snooper, Nancy Drew," Pierre spat. "If I'd known you were that smart, I'd have aimed that spear gun at you instead of her."

He raised the gun's muzzle with an icy chuckle. "Maybe I'll have better luck with this, eh?" He tilted his head at the cabin. "Inside, both of you. Now!"

Nancy had lost her first wager, but she would never give up hope. As she followed Bree through the hatchway she said as bravely as she could, "You can't get away. The police know just as much as I do."

"I've got nothing to lose, if you're telling the truth." Pierre shoved Nancy onto the settee. "They've already got me for two murders. Two more won't make any difference."

Keeping the girls covered, Pierre started up the boat's engines. His free hand spun the steering wheel to starboard.

"I believe you two are about to have a little accident." Pierre pushed the thrust levers forward. The engine roared.

"Like the one you prepared for Tayo?" cried Bree angrily.

"Something like that." Pierre's grin was cold. "I thought I had it all worked out. I forgot about the anchor, though. Tayo didn't—too bad for him! I thought I was home free." He scowled at Bree. "Then you came back to Tahiti. There'll be no slip-ups *this* time!"

Glancing over her shoulder, Nancy looked through the porthole. Arue's waterfront receded steadily, obscured by rolling whitecaps.

Bree began to sob.

Nancy took her hand and squeezed it. "Don't. We're not beaten yet."

"I—I was thinking of my father," Bree whispered tearfully. "I was so *wrong!* I was so unfair to him and Kristin. And now I'll never get the chance to apologize."

"We'll see about that," Nancy whispered. "Just keep your eyes and ears open, Bree. And be ready to follow my lead."

Ten minutes later Pierre cut power to the engines. The boat rolled in the trough of the waves. Crossing the cabin, he jerked his gun muzzle at a pile of scuba gear. "Carry that out on deck! Quick!"

Nancy made certain that she grabbed the air tanks. A desperate plan was beginning to take shape in her mind. It was a very long shot, she knew, but it was all she had.

Pierre ordered Bree to suit up. She obeyed, donning the gear like the expert she was. Her fearful eyes stayed riveted to the gun. Then he told Nancy to put on a pair of flippers. Nancy did as she was told, then slipped one of the air tanks into Bree's harness.

As she hooked up the regulator, Nancy asked coolly, "How do you plan to work it this time?"

Pierre smiled thinly. "Bree went diving and got into trouble. You put on those flippers and jumped in to save her. You both drowned."

Nancy picked up the second compressed air tank. Suddenly she turned to face Pierre, the nozzle of the air tank aimed at his face.

His smile vanished as a jet of compressed air exploded in his eyes.

"Bree! Over the side! Quick!" Nancy called. She kept her thumb on the valve, blinding Pierre with a stinging blast of air. There was a bang as his gun fired wildly into the air.

Dropping the tank, Nancy followed her friend. She reached the gunwale in two seconds and launched herself into the sea like an Olympic diving champion. Long overhead strokes carried her away from the boat.

Just ahead, Bree treaded water, waving frantically. "Nancy, dive! I'll meet you below!"

A rain of bullets kicked up miniature fountains

on either side of Nancy. Taking a deep breath, she plunged into an oncoming wave.

Soup-warm water enveloped her. Kicking from the waist, Nancy propelled herself into the depths. Bree swam toward her, a silhouette in a universe of turquoise light. Slipping the bubbling air regulator from her mouth, she offered it to Nancy.

Grateful, Nancy took a lifesaving breath. Buddy-breathing off the same tank, they could stay under for almost an hour.

They passed the regulator back and forth. Bree pulled insistently on Nancy's forearm, tugging her out to sea.

Minutes later Nancy heard a burbling splash-down behind them. Turning, she saw Pierre beneath the boat's hull, scuba rig on his back, spear gun in his hands. Spying the girls, he moved quickly, a line of bubbles trailing behind him.

Nancy swam deeper and faster, Bree at her side. Water pressure squeezed her eyeballs. Nancy took a long breath from Bree's mouthpiece, then kicked with a powerful, rhythmic stroke.

Ahead, the seabed dipped into a black sand hollow, overgrown with kelp. In the center lay an old Liberty ship left after World War II. The wreck lay on its side, a jagged torpedo crater in her rusting hull. Bree headed straight for it.

Just then, a spear rushed overhead.

Missed us! Nancy thought, but her relief was short-lived. They weren't the target at all!

Pierre's spear struck a yellowfin. The fish writhed in agony. Blood stained the water a dark crimson.

An ominous shadow crossed the sand in front of Nancy.

She looked up. Her stomach felt as if it were full of icicles. The true purpose of Pierre's long-range shot became frighteningly clear.

A school of gray reef sharks cruised near the surface. The scent of blood reached them. One by one, they broke formation and zoomed into the depths.

Terror paralyzed Nancy's every nerve. She watched helplessly as the blood-crazed sharks speeded toward them. Jagged teeth gleamed as they closed in for the kill!

Chapter

Seventeen

Bᴙᴇᴇ's ʜᴀɴᴅ ᴛᴜɢɢɪɴɢ ᴀᴛ Nancy shattered her momentary paralysis. Taking a quick breath from the mouthpiece, she joined Bree in a frantic descent to the bottom.

Nancy swam desperately, not daring to look back. Fatigue launched painful spasms down her arms and legs. At any moment she expected to feel the slash of a shark's teeth.

A narrow pilothouse window loomed ahead.

Suddenly Bree's hand jerked out of Nancy's grip. Turning, she saw Bree thrashing about. Her eyes bulged in horror. There was a shark at Bree's foot.

The shark had sunk its teeth into Bree's flipper. It shook its head back and forth, chewing the tough rubber the way a puppy tears at a rolled-up newspaper. Bree kicked it savagely in the gills with her free foot. The shark veered away, a semicircular chunk of rubber in its mouth.

But others were closing in fast.

Nancy pushed Bree through the open window, then dived through it head-first herself. A huge shark zoomed past the window frame, missing Nancy by mere seconds.

Nancy and Bree ducked into the ship's inside corridor. Bree pulled the hatch shut. After giving Nancy another breath of air, she led the way down the topsy-turvy corridor.

Nancy trailed her into a small stateroom. Bree ascended abruptly and Nancy followed.

To her astonishment, Nancy's head broke water. The air had a saline reek, but it was breathable. The chill stung her face.

"Where are we?" Nancy gasped.

Bree removed her mouthpiece. "In an air pocket. When she was torpedoed and sank, air got trapped in a few of the staterooms. Tayo showed me this place."

"How deep are we?" Nancy asked.

Bree's face tensed thoughtfully. "Fifty feet, I think. So if I remember my dive tables correctly, we can stay down here for forty minutes without getting the bends."

"Pierre will be here long before then," Nancy said, teeth chattering. "But maybe we can take him by surprise."

"What do you mean?"

"Pierre expects us to stay together. If we split, I might be able to sneak up on him," Nancy explained. "Bree, are you willing to play decoy?"

"What do you want me to do?"

"Show me how to get to the torpedo hole from here," Nancy suggested. "Then you go aft and make a break for the surface. I'll try to jump him—"

"Without an air tank?" cried Bree.

"It's our only chance!" Nancy shook her head stubbornly. "Please, Bree, you've got to make a break for it. Don't worry about me. I've been in tough spots before."

Maybe never quite *this* tough, she admitted to herself.

"What are you going to do for air?" Bree asked. "You'll never make it back here on just one breath."

"Give me your knife," Nancy pleaded, extending her open palm. "I'll cut Pierre's air hose when I come up behind him and steal my air from him."

Bree looked at Nancy for a long moment. "I hope you know what you're doing." Then, lifting her leg out of the water, she withdrew her knife from its ankle sheath. Nancy quickly averted her gaze from Bree's savagely torn flipper. No point in adding to her worries now!

After Bree had ducked beneath the surface, Nancy clutched a salt-caked lampstand and forced herself to relax. Long, slow breaths soothed her quivering muscles. With only one chance at this, she had to do it right.

Filling her lungs to the brim, Nancy submerged again.

Her eyes adjusted quickly to the dark blue water. Swimming with a rhythmic breaststroke, she left the stateroom and started down the corridor. Tiny bubbles escaped her taut lips.

All at once Nancy stopped short. Waving her arms to keep her balance, she stayed motionless in the water. Something was moving up ahead. Something *huge!*

Nancy watched in horror as an enormous shark emerged from the shadows. It was too big to be a reef shark—then Nancy glimpsed its pale underbelly. A great white!

The huge predator, ten feet from nose to tail, drifted down the corridor. Its movements told her it hadn't yet sensed her presence.

Nancy looked desperately in all directions, but solid walls hemmed her in. She was trapped. And the great white shark was headed straight her way.

Suddenly Nancy's gaze zeroed in on an empty tool locker. She drifted toward it slowly and deliberately, taking care not to stir up the water.

Slipping inside, she flattened against the locker's back wall, willing her shaking body to keep still.

As nearsighted as a bat, the giant shark swam by. His heavy body jolted the locker. A fin grazed Nancy's legs.

Keep going! Nancy wanted to scream. Keep going!

Her lungs began to burn. Her oxygen was running out fast. Heart beating madly, she watched as the shark's long length glided past.

The shark disappeared into the corridor's gloom. Relief invigorated Nancy's weary limbs. Plunging out of the locker, she rocketed down the corridor, trying to ignore the fire in her lungs.

Seconds slipped by. Nancy swam as fast as her limbs would carry her. Pierre's air tank was her only salvation now.

Nancy was choking. Red mist encircled her field of vision. Her lungs throbbed agonizingly. Only a few seconds of air remained.

The torpedo hole sent a shaft of turquoise light into the ship. Nancy swam straight for it. She popped out of the hull like a runaway cork, looking everywhere at once.

Pierre floated several feet away, his back to Nancy, taking aim with his spear gun. Fifty yards away, Bree was soaring to the surface.

Swimming up behind him, Nancy grabbed Pierre around the head. Bubbles exploded from where her knife severed his air hose. Nancy snatched the writhing hose and helped herself to a life-giving swallow.

Dropping his spear gun, Pierre tried to push her away. Nancy ripped his face mask off. Pierre's outflung fist knocked Nancy's knife away. They wrestled ferociously, then Pierre brought his strength to bear. Thick-muscled arms hurled Nancy away.

Nancy drifted backward, hitting the hull. She watched helplessly as Pierre stooped for his spear gun.

All of a sudden a grayish white torpedo zoomed out of the jagged hole. Nancy blinked in alarm. *The shark!*

The great fish struck Pierre heavily. Limp, he drifted to the seabed, unconscious.

Nancy swam over and grabbed the spear gun. The threat of attack was still horrifyingly real. She tried not to think of the shark's razor-sharp teeth as she took aim, her forefinger tight on the trigger.

Her shot grazed the great fish's side. For a terrifying moment, it continued to come toward her, its savage eyes unblinking. Then suddenly it veered away, speeding toward the open sea. The other sharks, scenting fresh blood, followed in a long string.

Nancy had no time for celebration. Her lungs were throbbing again. Tossing aside the spear gun, she swam over to Pierre and took another breath from his bubbling air hose.

Then, sipping air from his tank, Nancy hauled the unconscious man to the surface.

The water shifted color, from turquoise to sapphire to pastel blue. With a gasp of thanksgiving, Nancy broke the surface. Fresh air had never tasted so sweet!

The rumble of boat engines caught Nancy's

ear. The *Sous le Vent* coasted to a stop nearby. Bree appeared at the gunwale. Relief lit up her face.

"Nancy! You're all right!"

"More or less!" Nancy spit out a mouthful of seawater. "Give me a hand with Pierre, huh?"

Together they hauled him on deck. Nancy gave him artificial respiration. After several moments he coughed up seawater. Then, with a soft moan, he began to breathe normally.

Nancy rolled him over and bound his wrists with a short length of nylon cord.

"I swam to the boat as soon as I reached the surface," Bree said, covering Nancy's shoulders with a dry towel. "But when I got here, I saw shark fins. I thought—"

"Please don't," Nancy interrupted. She drew a deep breath. "We'd better call the police."

"There's a ship-to-shore radio up forward, just above the helm," Bree offered.

"Thanks!" Dizzy with fatigue, her lungs still aching, Nancy pulled herself to her feet.

Two days later Nancy stood in the lush garden of Faretaha. Guests crowded around the bonfire as the chef roasted a pig. Nearby a trio of Tahitian women performed the *tamure*, the island's famous hip-shaking folk dance.

Then Nancy noticed one unsmiling face in the crowd. Bree Gordon stood alone on the terrace, looking sadly out to sea.

Setting her glass of fruit punch aside, Nancy approached her. "Mind if I join you?"

Bree gave her a small smile. "Go ahead. You're welcome anytime." She seated herself on the low lava-rock wall. "I hear you were at the gendarmerie today."

Nancy nodded. "Captain Mutoi took my testimony. It's a busy courthouse. Rupert pleaded guilty to blackmail and extortion and got three years. Pierre goes to trial next month. The captain says he'll probably get life." She sat beside Bree. "I'm glad you and your father decided not to prosecute Manda."

Taking a deep breath, Bree replied, "Well, Dad and I had a long talk about that—among other things."

"And?"

"Dad was a lot more understanding than I thought he'd be," Bree said quietly. "And he's not a bit upset with me at all."

"Then why do you look so sad?"

"It's Kristin." Misery filled Bree's brown eyes. "I finally had a chance to apologize to her. She listened to me politely, gave me this cold look, and then walked away. I blew it, Nancy. She's never going to forgive me."

Nancy smiled in sympathy. "You know the old saying. Try, try again."

"Come on!" Bree glanced at her sharply. "Do you really think Krissy and I can ever be friends after *this?*"

"I don't know," Nancy replied. "Do you want to be friends with her?"

"I think I do." Bree's voice was thick with emotion. "I've seen how much she means to Dad. And she's not nearly as bad as I thought she was." She smiled sourly. "Know something? I think maybe I *wanted* Krissy to be guilty, so I could have an excuse to hate her." Looking away, she murmured, "I guess I wasn't that reconciled to their marriage, was I?"

"I guess not." Nancy put her arm over the girl's shoulders. "But you mustn't cut yourself off from them, Bree. That's the worst thing you could do. Kristin's going to be a part of your family. She needs your love and support just as much as your father does. You've got to be there to welcome her."

Bree's uncertain gaze traveled from Nancy to Kristin.

"I don't think she's going to be very pleased to see me."

"Maybe not at first," Nancy replied. "But give her time." She looked into Bree's eyes. "You two may never be as close as you and your mother were. But I think you can be friends. You just have to work at it."

"It's not possible."

"There you go again, jumping to conclusions!" Nancy replied, showing a small smile. "Don't close the case before you've even tried to solve it. Give it your best shot!"

The black-haired girl burst into laughter.

"When the advice comes from a real detective, it would be dumb not to listen, right?" Bree squeezed Nancy's hand thankfully. "Excuse me. I've got to go talk to my future stepmother."

Satisfied, Nancy looked away. Bree and Kristin could patch things up, she had no doubt.

Soft breezes stirred her hair. Leaning against the wall, she watched the full moon paint a silvery sword on the placid surface of the sea.

A masculine voice sounded behind her. "Mademoiselle Drew? You have a phone call."

"Thank you." Nancy followed the servant through the open French windows into the spacious parlor.

Picking up the receiver, she said, "This is Nancy Drew."

"Hi, Nancy!" Bess Marvin's voice exclaimed joyously. "I just couldn't wait to hear all about Tahiti!"

Grinning, Nancy began, "Well, there was this shark—"

"Nancy!" Bess complained. "I don't want to hear fish stories. I want to hear about the *guys!*"

Nancy's next case:

Ned invites Nancy to exclusive Basson College to meet his friend Linc Sheffield. But when they arrive, they discover Linc unconscious after suffering a nasty fall. His mumbled clues lead the teen detective to a number of skeletons in the school's closets. The most sinister is the mysterious "suicide" of popular Professor Evans. As Nancy digs deeper she finds herself in a desperate race to crack a computer code—and uncover a deadly secret in *HIGH MARKS FOR MALICE,* Case #32 in the Nancy Drew Files™.